THE HONEYMOON MIX-UP

SAPPHIRE ISLE BOOK 1

FRANKIE FYRE

Credits

Cover Design by Alt 19 Creative

Editing by Emma/Emerald Ink Editing

<u>Content Warning:</u>

On-page or Extensive Discussion:

- Explicit sex on page
- Graphic language
- Mother-daughter relationship issues

Off-page or Brief Mention:

- Loss of a parent
- Difficult IVF experience
- Bullying towards queer people

Note** Sapphire Isle is a *fictional* Sapphic island outside of Thailand.

For more information regarding content warning for any of Frankie's books, please contact her via her website.

ACKNOWLEDGEMENTS

My sweet Georgia peach, I love you dearly. Another book :D Thank you for always believing in my storytelling and in me especially during the times I struggle to believe in myself. Your support, kisses and love give me life.

My editor, Emma, thank you for your divine talents, laughs, encouragement and helping me grow. You're a beautiful soul.

Thank you for growing with me! <3

BLURB

The perfect storm. A fake marriage weathered to last.

When her fiancée leaves her at the altar, Basil Jones's picture perfect life turns upside down, but nothing can stop her from enjoying her honeymoon—not even the luxurious island resort's strict "couples only" policy. Basil's vacation and her six-figure wine deal with the resort's owners are riding on her finding a fake wife ASAP, and her sights are soon set on tall, dark, and gorgeous Caroline.

If only she knew Caroline had eyes on her first…

Caroline King never stays in one place—or in a woman's bed—for too long. After risking her career in the past, the emotionally detached private investigator created two rules: always finish a job and never mix business with pleasure.

But when she gets roped into a false marriage with her breathtakingly beautiful target, she finds herself teetering the line of not just one but both rules.

Basil always gets what she wants—but Caroline's professional reputation is on the line.

As Basil and Caroline's attraction blazes like the island sun, both women struggle to fight delicious temptation while protecting their secrets—as well as their hearts—on the most romantic honeymoon island in the world.

Each book in the Sapphire Isle series can be enjoyed as a standalone.

CHAPTER 1

BASIL

I THINK it was the third kiss that woke me—and not just from sleep. I'm catapulted back to reality. What in the hell am I still doing in this bed? With this woman? A total stranger.

The weight of the person who *isn't* Olivia rests on top of me. Warm, naked skin. Strong hands. Her taste on my lips. Murmured words brush along my spine and tiny moans escape my throat as a path of kisses reaches my earlobe. I'm more calm than I should be right now thanks to her soothing body heat. My shoulders relax and the agony from the last forty-eight hours—the disastrous wedding, the business deal, the bass from the music pounding my eardrums last night—melts away. Distant sounds of honking cars yanks my attention back to reality once more. I need to get out of here. *Look alive, Basil.*

"Morning," I mumble, fueled both with a desire to go another round and to leave this hotel immediately. *Stupid.* The rooftop party was a terrible idea, especially in downtown Seattle. What if someone from the office saw us acting like a couple of horny college kids?

My thoughts redirect as tingles travel south from the

weight of her breasts pressing firmly against my back in the same manner her lips sank into my neck on the dance floor. And now I crave her touch again. Fuck. Why does my body keep betraying me? When she lifts herself and hovers over me, I roll between her long arms to face her. My heart jumps at the warmth of her smile.

She's even more beautiful in the natural light. I smile at the voluminous dark coils of her hair. The morning sun peeking through the sheer curtains forces me to shift my focus from her grin to the light illuminating the smoothness of her copper brown complexion. She leans closer and says "Good morning." Her whispered words compel my body to respond, and next thing I know, my lips are pressed against the hollow part near her forearm. Her warm leg nestles between my thighs, and she flashes me a look. I recall the exact moment last night I knew I wanted her. *Her...*What's her name again? I can't remember, and hell no, I'm not going to ask. I don't do this type of thing. Hooking up.

I clear my throat, interrupting my thoughts before I lose myself completely. "What time is it? My flight—" I pause and think better of opening myself up for questions. It might not be wise to confess you were just left at the altar and decided to go on your honeymoon alone while a naked woman is on top of you. Instead, I do what I shouldn't and run my hands down her toned sides, letting everything about her pull me back in. The urge to stay here forever, to forget the shitshow that is my life, is overwhelming, but—no, I can't. No giving in to this conflicting ache in my chest for something I know will never happen between us. Jones women don't get the luxury of sustaining impulse decisions unless they produce money. Our eyes hold, and she dips down and kisses me— not where I want, but gently on my forehead—then glances toward the nightstand.

"Ten till 7 a.m." Her voice is soothing yet commanding.

She maneuvers toward the edge of the bed and sits up. "Have somewhere to be?"

I should already be at the airport. My *international* flight leaves in less than three hours. Hell, I haven't even checked in yet. The sinking sensation in my stomach plummets to my core. The satisfaction of last night has faded. This woman has no clue who I am. A distraction from a day gone horribly wrong. And I was probably just another notch in her bedpost. I'm single—after *seven years*, but it feels like I'm married, making this situation much worse.

As she slides her sports bra over her head and adjusts it into place, I point my gaze toward the wall for a faux sense of privacy, then wrap the sheets over my chest and rest on my elbows. I take a deep breath and wait to retrieve my scrambled clothes littering the room.

Before I realize I didn't answer the question, she breaks the silence. "You know, if you want to leave, that's fine."

"No. It's not that. I, um—" I peer around and scan my mind for an excuse. "With all our dancing…in and out of the bedroom…I'm all out of fuel. Know of any good breakfast spots around here? I'm thinking perhaps a pastry, maybe some coffee." Then I lie. "I'm not from the area."

She squints and tilts her head with a quizzical expression, like she wants to say something, but she hesitates. "There's a bakery next door. I'm told they have great coffee too."

I'm told? My sight dances up and down her tall, fit frame. With a body like that, she probably takes all her one-night stands there. I force a smile. "Perfect. I'll have a vanilla chai latte with a shot of espresso. Smallest they have is fine. Thanks." A silent moment passes, and I catch her raised brow pointing in my direction through the mirror. "What?"

"So, a dirty vanilla chai?" The corner of her mouth curls.

I chuckle, not bothering to hide the hint of sarcasm and cross my arms over my chest. "Not the same thing."

"It absolutely is."

"I know coffee." Mine gets delivered to my desk every day at 8 a.m. "It's not."

"Yes, it—" She pauses and blinks twice. "I actually meant for us to go together." Then she points a finger up. "Also, last night you mentioned you got your clothes from the local boutique downtown."

I can see my black lace panties on the chair arm through the mirror, but I don't draw attention to them. "They were a gift." Technically, that's not a lie. An early wedding present, intended to be a surprise for Olivia.

Thankfully, she turns to search for her jeans, but just when I think the topic is dropped, she continues, "And that you *love* shopping there. Wait. Was last night not good for you?"

This woman asks too many questions. Our eyes meet, and my face heats up when I remember all the dirty little promises she made good on. "Did I seem like I didn't enjoy last night?"

No response, but her devious smirk tells me we're probably thinking the same thing. Great. It's official: I don't care if I'm only thirty, I refuse to have a one-night stand again. I wouldn't survive modern-day dating. There's no point in trying.

"So, a dirty vanilla chai then?" A big smile crosses her face, and she disappears into the bathroom.

"I liked it better when we weren't talking," I mutter a little too loud. I need her gone to gather my thoughts and my belongings. The clock is ticking. I've never missed a flight before and don't intend to start now.

From the other room, she yells over the running faucet, "I'm sorry, I missed what you said."

I roll my eyes, impatience getting the best of me. Instead of responding right away, I fling the sheets off and scramble for my clothes. As I stand, words to shout back strike my mind. "I said, I'd rather stay here and wait for you—" The water stops, and she darts her head through the doorway, those big brown eyes staring and a toothbrush dangling from her teasing grin at my stark nakedness. I'm hot all over and speechless when she gives me a once-over.

"Just like that?" She raises a brow, then disappears again. "In that case, maybe we should skip the bakery."

Is she toying with me? I can't tell. I'm only stuck wondering how a woman could be so damn attractive while brushing her teeth.

We finish getting dressed and are standing in the main room. I peer down at my green blouse and pants that are wrinkled as hell—and don't get me started on the bird's nest on top of my head. I groan, directing my thoughts back to my flight to Sapphire Isle, and quickly pull my hair into a ponytail.

The woman, whose name I still don't know, lingers near the front door as if she just walked me home from an actual date—not a one-night stand. Should I be giving a code word or jingling my keys or something?

I hear her cell phone ring on the counter beside me, and I hand it over, unable to stop myself from seeing the name on the bright screen. She rushes to turn off the ringer and shoves the phone in her pocket. *Kaydence?* Did I just sleep with someone who's in a relationship?

Don't even go there.

"Thanks." She grins at the floor. "Work thing. I'll call her back later." After opening the door, she turns to look at me. "I know we agreed on no names last night—well, you know mine—anyway, I was wondering if I could know yours."

She seems sincere enough for me to want to tell her, but it's futile. We will never see each other again. I rack my brain for a moment. "How about..." The scent of the cool mint on

5

her breath draws me forward, and something in my stomach flutters. As I drift closer, I catch myself from kissing her, our lips hovering centimeters away. "I'll tell you when you get back."

She flashes me that daring, seductive look I recall from across the rooftop. "Bet."

I return a smile, and a few seconds later, she's gone.

After letting five minutes pass, I slowly pull the door open, luggage in hand, and check that the coast is clear. Time to finally leave this hotel. Time to close this wine deal before my boss—a.k.a. my mother—passes me up for promotion. Again. I have two weeks on a luxury island to get my life together. I don't have time for heartbreak, only money and mojitos. *Look alive, Basil.*

I enter the elevator down the hall. One last glance at the door, the one she pressed me up and kissed me against for the first time. "Bye, Caroline..." Her name escapes my lips in a whisper before I press the button, relieved that at least I remember the woman's name whose touch I'll never forget.

CHAPTER 2

CAROLINE

"DAMN IT, KAYDENCE," I grumble at the insistent ringing from my pocket. My hands are full, and this is the third time she's called since I left the bakery. In pursuit of my phone, I nearly paint the sidewalk with both lattes before halting at the bench outside the hotel. The paper bag plops on the black steel right before my "one of everything" order tumbles to the ground. Too focused on the brunette from last night, I forgot to inquire about her food preferences. Honestly, I'm surprised I'm buying a woman breakfast at all.

I sit and answer the fourth ring. "King speaking."

There's a playful buzzing sound on the other end. "Don't get that formal tone with me, King. Don't you know it's National Assistant Day?"

That makes me laugh. "You say that every time you call me on a weekend. Besides, I'd hardly say you're an assistant. More like a glorified front desk receptionist who's never available," I tease.

"Unfortunately, not this time." Her chuckle deflates into a long sigh. "Remind me again why I agreed to take all client communication? You know it's a bad day when the side hustle is hectic enough to make my soul-sucking day job look good. Can't believe I'm saying this, but I miss the field."

"I'll gladly take you back in a heartbeat. Don't expect cybersecurity money though." I prefer working solo, but Kaydence is the only person I can tolerate for ten hours in a car if need be. When we did work cases together, it was mostly her whining about the amount of takeout I forged through. And I complained about her loud singing before changing the radio station. I miss our dynamic duo sometimes. "Make sure you clear it with the wife."

"Denied. I'd rather not go there."

"Thought so." I reminisce about when it all began. The day I left the federal government agency and took the leap of starting my own private investigation business—that intimidating level of independence back then is now a necessity. Kaydence was the first and only person I hired. She has played a pivotal role in my success as a PI for what? Twenty years now? Even after swapping forensic cases for a corporate nine-to-five, she stuck around to assist with audits and clients. One thing she'll never understand is how appreciative I am to never have to speak to a client again, especially after Grace.

"As much as I'd love to join you, you know I can't." She rambles her whys—a reminder, more for herself than me. "One: I made a commitment to show up for my kids. Two: I love being happily married. The day I miss one of Rosie's Jiu-Jitsu classes, we're both rightfully dead. You're just going to have to let me live vicariously through you. Minus your ten 'only down for fun' dating accounts."

"Two, and I barely use one," I say matter-of-factly and brush the judgment away. Why do married queers act like everyone around them needs the piece of paper too? After all, I am a whole-ass adult. Who is constantly on the road for work. Who doesn't have time for money problems or couples

therapy or bold-faced lies. I don't need anyone else to be happy. "Wasn't it you that told me to get out more? 'Take a fresh-air vacation. No working inside your car'? Well, that's what I am doing."

"Fresh air…in the *city*? I hope you felt that eye roll."

I can't help but grin. "Sure did."

"Back to the matter at hand. There are only two possible reasons you refuse to answer on the first call. Either surveillance is heating up or you're fuc—" Her voice drops to a whisper. "Ducking. And since I *know* you're not in the field, which is it? Please say you finally called Elle."

Something down the street steals my attention. "Hold on, Kaydence." I excuse myself, my gaze trailing the cyclist peering down at his phone and hauling full speed in my direction. A city bus driver who's clearly not paying attention to his mirrors cuts into traffic. The cyclist dodges and loses both control and the phone, but manages to stay upright. Close call. I release my held breath and shake my head. *People be peopling.* My nose wrinkles when I inhale the remnants of exhaust and stale beer. Maybe Kaydence is right about getting some fresh air. Seattle, being one of the cleaner-smelling cities I've lived in, can still have an odor in the mornings that leaves something to be desired.

Returning to the conversation, I stretch my legs and tilt my head back. "I'm not with Elle." No matter how many times I tell Kaydence I'm not interested in her matchmaking services, her stubbornness persists. We have that in common, like with most things, except I swear by my intuition while she insists on trusting data. Both end up being utilized at the end of the day. She challenges me nonetheless. It's also why we've been friends since boot camp. "I told you, I don't need to go on a date with someone to know we aren't a good fit. I'm notably discerning these days."

"Discerning or unwilling to trust?"

Both. And that's an understatement. I pivot the conversation. "If you must know, I went to a rooftop party last night. The After Pride After-Party I told you about."

A groan echoes through the speaker. Hearing rapid taps on a keyboard, I can picture Kaydence lost in focus, her face an inch away from the screen. After slamming the last key a moment later, she responds. "I should be jealous of the fun, but my body aches on your behalf. I don't know how you keep up with all that drinking and dancing in your forties. I'm over here at thirty-three, just trying to soak up all the sleep I can before the baby comes. Rosie's sleep regression has improved, but still."

She's said that like I'm pushing fifty—not the eight year difference. She knows I'm notoriously private. Meanwhile, she gossips more than anyone I know, only to tell her wife every detail later. Just because Kaydence sports the perfect fade haircut, spouse, and French bulldog, and has a kid with baby number two on the way, doesn't mean I have to follow suit. There are other options.

Cue the naked mystery woman upstairs waiting for me.

A glance at my watch tells me it's been over twenty minutes. Too bad I spent nearly ten of them contemplating the menu. Better get going. Remembering my Bluetooth headphones in my pocket, I shove one in my right ear. I stand and grab the food, and with a latte in each hand, I pace toward the room. Since I missed my morning run, I settle on taking the four flights of stairs. "You have three minutes until I hang up this phone and return to my plans from last night."

"Ha! I knew you charmed a woman with your tall-ass dapper self."

"And yes, before you start lecturing me about safe sex, I got tested before and will get tested after. Discussed the matter with her too."

"Happy to help." Kaydence laughs. "Case details later. You know the drill."

My brows pinch together. *The Four Ws and H*. What a ridiculous pastime activity we started during our months in Germany. "Seriously? We're still doing that dumb game?"

"Come on, it's been either *A Goofy Movie* or *The Princess and the Frog* for three days straight."

"My god daughter has great taste in movies. She didn't get that from you." I laugh.

"You're right. That's all Nikita there. Seriously, though. I need *some* entertainment."

"Fair enough. You're lucky I stepped out for food, otherwise I'd say no." Passing the second floor landing, I add a pep to my step, jogging two stairs at a time. Thank you, long legs. Deep breath…and *go*.

"Who?" Kaydence fires question one.

"Don't know her name yet." I peeked at her luggage tag this morning, but only caught the initials 'B. H. J.' She claims to not be from Seattle, but three articles of clothing and her heels were from a local boutique. Either she lied, or she at least has family from the area.

"What positions?"

"*None* of your business." I chuckle, reaching the last flight of stairs. "In the bed…mostly.

"When?"

"Last night.

"Weapon of destruction?"

"Eyes." I've never seen ocean-blue eyes like hers before.

"Wearing what?"

"Heels, skinny jeans, and a low-cut top. Above average height. Pink lipstick. White, brunette, wavy hair with auburn highlights. Dimple, right side." One more question.

"How bad do you want to see her again?"

The image of the softness of her lips on my neck brings a

smile to my face. Enough to buy her breakfast. Another thing that hasn't happened since Grace.

"I'm not certain yet. She looks easily ten years younger, and nothing against the younger women, but different phases of life and all that. She does seem a bit uptight, like she holds a high corporate position, but in an attractive, power-lesbian way."

"Very nice, King," she muses with enthusiastic clapping as always. "You certainly do have a type."

I do not. "It's nothing serious, just a one night thing," I emphasize, purposely leaving out the breakfast details. My brows pinch together. Maybe I should consider asking the mystery woman on a date after I learn her name. Now I'm curious about what Kaydence will say next. "Score?"

"Eh, I give it a 2 out of 10 probability she'll be there when you get back. I think you left the room for a reason."

My lips form a pout. Of course she would say that because of her preference for Team Elle. But what Kaydence doesn't know is that I have coffee for two. "Bet you a beer she will be." To prove my point, I add, "And if I said her name was Elle?"

"10 out of 10."

I burst out laughing. "Shut up, Jennings. Oh, that French bakery, Mr. B's, has seven types of croissants, *sixteen* tart flavors, nine different danishes, and five beignets. Ask me how I know." I pause in the fourth-floor hallway, shake my head at the paper bag in my arms, and change the subject before she gets the chance. "Do you have case details for me? Sixty seconds."

She returns to her professional composure and begins her briefing. "Rush job. A straightforward surveillance case. Your *favorite* client." Audible exhale. "You know, the one that's a royal pain in my ass. The one we've been working with for three years and still don't know more than her pronouns. You know I don't like getting bossed around by her liaison."

I sense another eye roll through the phone. Kaydence, reluctant when I took in this client, says a person who goes to such lengths for anonymity must be bad news. After what Grace did to me—and after what I did to myself—I disagree. "Clear boundaries don't make a client a pain in the ass." *Sleeping with them does,* I almost say, but don't. I'll never mix work with pleasure again.

"I got bad news. For me, anyway. The client advised instead of the liaison running the show, she'll be hands-on with this case, which makes me think it's personal. Your instructions are simple: Keep your distance and report back."

"She's one lady I wouldn't want to cross."

"The good news is, she's paying a pretty penny, *including* a vacation. An actual vacation that's not inside your car. Pack your bags, King: you're going to Sapphire Isle."

"Sounds familiar." I think for a moment, then recall the Autostraddle article Grace sent me once. Another promise that fell through. "That sapphic island outside of Thailand with a couple's resort? Did you scope out the place yet?"

"Yes and yes. I just sent your plane ticket to your inbox. I'm working on room and board as we speak. Once I get a few more details from the client, I'll send the case file over."

"Thank you." I reach the door and dig through my pocket for the room key. "How much time do I have?"

"Less than twenty-four hours."

"That's not the worst we've had for a rush job. Give me a few hours and I'll call you back."

I end the conversation and take a breath before opening the door. At least there's plenty of time with—

The room is empty. She's gone. Damn. I hate it when Kaydence is right.

CHAPTER 3

BASIL

BREAKING bad news to my fiancée on our wedding day wasn't the worst decision I've ever made. Okay, *fine*. Harboring the news for weeks and *then* telling my future wife, who had her head buried between my legs on the morning of our wedding—*that* might take the cake. A real Basil Jones victory.

So what if I needed to do a little work on our honeymoon? People did that all the time…didn't they? That doesn't justify dumping someone at the—

"Another mojito, Ms. Jones?" The flight attendant appears out of thin air.

I flinch. "For fuck's sake." I press pause on *John Wick*, after having restarted the movie for the fourth time. Knocking back the drink in my hand, I push the empty cup away and nod for another.

"People take solo vacations all the time, right?" I ask, hand bumping my cup, almost spilling the lingering drops on her skirt, before I watch my next drink being poured.

"Of course! We see it a lot, actually." Her irritatingly bright smile points in my direction.

I flash a thin one back, then glance at the empty first-class window seat to my right. "But I mean, probably not their honeymoons..." My eyes widen when I realize the words came out louder than intended. I divert my gaze toward the shadows of the clouds as we shift altitude.

The flight attendant sets the drink down and pauses, an awkward silence stretching between us. When I turn to thank her, I catch the tail end of her blank stare before she bolts down the aisle.

"Go ahead, leave. They all do anyway." I squint a glare, then slam my back against the plush seat and shift from side to side. First class isn't nearly as comfortable as I remember, or perhaps the fabric changes when you're newly single. I resume the movie only to pause the screen again ten minutes later.

I give up.

As I tip the plastic cup back against my lips, scents of sugar, lime and fresh mint meet my nose. The alcohol warms its way down my throat, spreading to my toes and fingertips, until I am no longer able to taste the bite of rum.

The heaviness in my eyes deepens as my glare burns a hole into the side pocket of my bag resting between my feet. The same bag Olivia's father gave me as a birthday gift three years ago. I'll miss his warm, dopey smile—the one thing he and Olivia share. Olivia. What happened to us? I reach for the zipper and pull out my engagement ring. I slide the white gold onto my finger and stare, chest tightening, as if the ring should no longer fit perfectly since the woman who gave it to me doesn't. No note? Did she cheat on me, leave me for someone else? How dare she make a fool out of me and my family's wine business. And after all she and I have been through? Maybe I was wrong about her—but for seven years?

A wave of lava flows through my body as I recall the

amount of planning involved to ensure we'd have the best honeymoon experience. This will not go to waste, even if my wedding did. Eyes on the island brochure nestled in the seat pocket in front of me, I thumb the corner. I'll be damned if I skip this trip and its incredible amenities over a failed wedding. Who cares if I have to stay at the couples' resort alone? Plus, Sapphire Isle is the one damn place Olivia isn't.

With shaky hands and tattered breathing, I yank the ring off and clench it until my knuckles whiten. A piece of jewelry that signified eternity and promise, which now purges from my heart. While rage, while—*abandonment*—stirs through my veins. I straighten and run my fingers through my hair. One unfinished task stands between me and my luxurious vacation.

After the flight attendants stroll past with the drink cart, I stand, march toward the plane lavatory, and slam my spine against the door, swallowing back my nerves. Each bounce of turbulence drives through my legs as the plane ebbs and flows. I can't stand flying, but I breathe through the twists in my stomach, knowing it will end soon. When I sit on the closed toilet seat, the agonizing pit in my belly returns, along with fire. No words can change the reality, but at least I'm *finally* the hell away from Seattle. No more of my mother's overt grip on my life. Going on about her "blueprint"—my identity and, of course, her Jones legacy. At least for the time being, there will be no more unbearable questions from friends or family. Although a haze forms across my mind, the nagging voice still pierces through my heart: *What did you do to make her leave you, Basil?*

I huff. *What did I do?* The fact that my mother adores Olivia only makes matters worse. Well, now she can have her.

After a minute of meditative breathing, I force the tears away. *Look alive, Basil.* I thumb the invisible indent on my finger and lift the ring to eye level. My jaw tightens at the pain as I stand and lift the lid. No, this won't solve everything, but it is a damn good start.

I drop the five-carat diamond ring into the toilet and flush down the last memento of the old Basil Jones. No one will betray my trust again.

Commending my performance, I fling the door open, march back, and nestle in my large seat, feeling livelier than before—or maybe the rum has kicked in. I don't know or care. The airplane dings as the seatbelt sign illuminates and the captain announces, "Flight attendants, please prepare for our descent into Sapphire Isle. The local time is 12:10 p.m. The weather is beautiful with a temperature of 82 degrees Fahrenheit and skies as blue as the ocean you'll see beneath us. Will have you on the ground enjoying the island shortly."

* * *

When I step into the Goddess Lagoon Resort lobby, an enchanting ambiance sparkles around me. Serenity canvasses the pristine, white marble–floored space. The Greek goddess statues are laced with vibrant vines and the walls with pillars as wide as the grin forming across my face. An impressive blend of Thai and Greek decor. My smile widens to its furthest point when I stroll past the tree-shaped water fountain. A penniless one at that.

Warmth from the early-afternoon sun seeps through the revolving doors, providing reassurance that I made the right decision to go on my honeymoon alone. The lobby smells of fresh summer flowers, vanilla, and cardamom. I bask in what will be my new sanctuary for the next two weeks, which exudes a type of peace I've only witnessed on my screensaver. For a moment, stress and anxiety from the last several hours melts, loosening my back and shoulder muscles.

The check-in line is short, but not moving quickly enough. My jaw tightens at the couple in front of me. Is that necessary? Every thirty seconds, the baseball hat–wearing brunette giggles and pecks the woman holding her hand, which signals the curly-haired woman to kiss the brunette's fingers. Their longing gazes and loud giggling are over the top. What is taking so long?

I inhale a long breath. No need to be annoyed. Within ten minutes, I'll be lying in a king-sized bed with more pillows and security than any woman could ever provide. I tilt my chin higher, step closer to my destination, and plant my Louis Vuitton carry-on luggage over a glass square built into the floor. Tiny orange and white fish swim unphased by the foot traffic. It reminds me of the pet goldfish Hazel and I—more me than her, meticulously cared for as a child, until one day, our older brother, Finn, said Gilbert escaped down the toilet drain back to the ocean. The first budding sign I was doomed at keeping relationships alive. I shake my head and walk to the next available receptionist, a White woman with red hair and bright smile, waving in my direction.

"Welcome to the Goddess Lagoon Resort. We're so delighted to have you stay with us. Could you please remind me of your name?" She stands with a cheerful, almost genuine disposition.

I nod, eagerly lifting my driver's license and printed confirmation paper. Something I like to bring in case technology fails me. A contingency plan, since my love life doesn't have one. I smooth the single wrinkle from the sheet and slide both items across the bamboo countertop. A wide grin settles on my face as I check the arrow-shaped signs. *Café. Restaurant. Event Hall. Gift Shop. Villas.* This is the final stop before beginning my recovery from the jetlag.

Rapid taps from long fingernails striking a keyboard echo

through the nearly empty room. I turn my attention back to the source.

The receptionist puts a hand over her heart. "Aww, congratulations. Honeymooners are so beautiful. Two women celebrating their marriage hits me hard right in the feels every time. Ugh. One day."

I force a smile. *Wonderful.* One of those "love conquers all" types. Hundreds of customers check in each week, so the exaggerated, awestruck performance is quite unnecessary. *Don't do it,* I start to say, but change my mind. Instead, a fake appreciative chuckle leaves my lips as I eye my golden ticket —the villa key—tucked inside the pocket of the brochure. I swear every redhead I know speaks too damn much. Aunt Patricia, my client William, and Jill—although she was a fantastic tennis partner.

"Thank you." I bat my eyes, pretending to care while she yammers on about the resort's package and couple activities I've replaced with sunbathing.

Once the spiel ends, she fixes her sights on my luggage bag, then back on me. "I just need your signatures and you are all set. Any questions?"

I place the ID and useless itinerary inside my bag. "No. This all sounds lovely, thank you."

"We also offer scheduled tours of the resort, given by yours truly. If that's of any interest to you."

I slide the paperwork back and shift my stance, picking at dots of lint on my sleeve. She didn't seem to like the way I dismissed her previous comment, but I don't care. This has to be over soon.

A weighted stare makes me look up.

"I just need your wife's signature and you'll be all set." Her tone is clipped.

Wife's signature? The blood drains from my face before a flash of heat replaces it. *Are you fucking kidding me right now?*

A couple walking through the entrance yanks my attention away, giving me just enough time to hide my gritting teeth. *Damn you, Olivia.* Not a single person will stand in the way of my six-figure wine contract or the king-sized bed with plush 1000-thread-count Egyptian cotton sheets. I smile wide at— name tag check—Sunny. And what a ray of sunshine she is.

"Hi, Sunny. I simply adore that name." After dialing up the charm, I continue, "Just curious, why do you need my wife's signature? Especially since I am the one who made the reservation."

"I'm terribly sorry for the inconvenience, Mrs. Jones." Sunny looks over my left shoulder, then my right, and does that rambling thing again. "We have a couples-only policy— well, it's technically *not* couples only. All types of sapphic relationships are welcome at Goddess Lagoon. Due to the increase in demand, we require all parties' signatures upon check-in. This information was located at the bottom of your reservation page when you booked. Line fif—"

"I read the reservation." Jesus. The *one* time I didn't fully review the paperwork before signing.

"*Okay.*" Sunny blinks. "Then you also read about our one-night grace period and cancellation policy. I understand you booked quite a while ago and may have forgotten. When will your wife get in?"

Question of the century. I chomp down on my tongue when I catch Sunny's fake grin, preventing me from giving her a piece of my mind. Haven't I been through enough for one lifetime? I cross my arms over my chest, searching for my next words. Keeping my voice steady is becoming a challenge, and she seems to love it. "The reason my wife will not be present today is because she has to deal with an emergency. A...logistics emergency and will arrive tomorrow morning." There. Done. I just need to get past this hell demon and the rest will be history.

Her features soften, bringing a slow smile to my lips. "How unfortunate." She straightens her back. "Please have her swing by the front desk when she arrives tomorrow and we'll get that signature from her."

I can work around that. We were enjoying our honeymoon *so* much it slipped our minds. *How unfortunate.* I quickly nod while extending the handle of my carry-on in victory, but halt at the next sobering words.

"It's due tomorrow. Otherwise, the system flags the account, and I'll have to ask you to leave. It's an island. We'll find you."

My eye twitches at her cute, evil chuckle.

The way Sunny replicates my eyelash flutter and her condescending smile irritates me all over again. I clear my throat. Fake it until you make it, I suppose. "In a situation where my wife's flight is delayed, what is the protocol? Paying customers should not be penalized for what is entirely out of our control." I know that all too well. Intertwining my fingers together, I wait for a response. Heat tingles my cheeks as whispers sound behind me. It looks like I'm making a scene. Well, Jones women don't do anything half-heartedly.

Sunny opens her mouth, and before letting her finish, I interject. "In fact, I'd like to speak with your manager to resolve this disarray. My important meeting with the owners —the Blakemans—is coming up, and I'm exhausted. Discussing my mediocre customer experience would be a waste of everyone's time. Therefore, I'm certain management would make an exception."

"With all due respect, those same owners were the ones who put this policy in place." She glances at the clock. "Unfortunately, my supervisor just stepped into a meeting. We understand life happens and navigating flights to the island can be a challenge, hence the grace period. You will be able to terminate your reservation and only be required to pay for the night, plus a thirty-percent surcharge to the card on file. Would you like to hear details regarding our cancellation policy?"

"No," I growl without a second thought. Going back to Seattle without executing this wine deal is simply not an option. "Like I said, we are celebrating our honeymoon, and my meeting with the owners of *this* establishment will not be impacted by your negligence." I grumble through gritting teeth, "My wife will be here tomorrow."

"Working during your honeymoon. Interesting." Another mocking smile tugs at her lips. "I look forward to meeting Mrs. Jones."

"I'm sure you do." My death grip on my carryon handle tightens, and I stroll toward the elevator, gaze pointing downward toward the fish judging me inside the floor.

A group of women step off the elevator. Their booming laughter seems to be aimed at me. How am I going to get that signature? Telling the Blakemans the truth isn't going to happen. Facing yet another embarrassment is not an option. I need a wife and *fast*. I shake my head and chuckle to myself. Hell, if I'd known, I would've asked that woman from the rooftop party. Ignoring the empty elevator, I scan the lobby, eyes halting on the concierge bag drop-off. I wheel my luggage over and request my bag be placed inside my villa. The short-haired Thai woman wearing a bowtie, who appears to be having a much better day than I am, brightens at the large tip I slide into her hands. At least someone's day is improving.

Light-bulb moment. I, Basil Jones, am charismatic, a knockout, and...*single*—sort of. I'll fix those details later. A two-week solo trip to an island is what I need, and redemption, fun, and more damn mojitos are what I deserve. After flashing a toothy grin, I ask the million-dollar question.

"Where is your closest bar?"

CHAPTER 4

CAROLINE

I YAWN, peering up at the wooden bar sign, *The Tiki Taco*, and enter the hut, crossing the threshold for shade. The thatch roof serves as a minuscule shield from the island's morning rays. At my last layover, Kaydence said she'd email the case details, but I haven't received them yet. I'm already behind, with check-in being hours away, and I have no file to review.

The sound of rushing waves washing over the seashell-littered sand helps loosen the stiffness in my neck muscles. I'll take this over a maddening rush hour any day. I breathe in, filling my lungs with the smell of crisp, clean air, and near the end catch a whiff of burning charcoal, paprika, and fresh garlic from the grill. The bartender, an Asian woman with midnight hair flowing to the middle of her back, walks over to take my order.

"Does your orange juice have light or no pulp?" I ask, opting in for an ocean-view seat in the empty bar. I drop my bag on the barstool beside me.

She nods. "Fairly light for fresh squeezed." A curious smile splits her lips. "Usually, patrons are more concerned with the amount of champagne that goes in, not the pulp."

I chuckle. "Hearing the word 'champagne' this early makes my stomach hurt. I'll take a glass of OJ, please."

"Coming right up." She points at a metal sign while lowering to open the mini fridge. *Tacos because murder is wrong.* "You're on a getaway island, and we serve food and alcohol twenty-four seven. There's no one judging around here if you change your mind." There's a contemplative sound. "Then again, after last night's debacle, I appreciate the change in pace."

"Debacle?" My eyebrows pinch together. Usually, I need to flirt to get insight from the locals, but not today, apparently. I'm not complaining. The last thing I want is to get involved with someone. My mind travels back to the empty hotel room in Seattle. See how well that turned out last time?

"Some teary-eyed woman going on about—I'm guessing her ex." She sets my drink in front of me. "Can't have an island filled with sapphics without dealing with relationship drama from time to time."

I take a sip and shrug. Paying local bars a visit often yields results and every once in a while, I'll sample the local cuisine. Food too. I open my mouth to inquire about the resort I'm staying at, Goddess Lagoon; however, hearing about someone else's relationship issues is oddly satisfying. I set my glass on the napkin square and rest my head on my fist. "What's the story there?"

The bartender points at a seat three down from me. "No clue, but she seemed like the *Dynasty* rich-bitch type. Sat right there and silently nursed drinks, which unraveled into a complete shitshow until I cut her off. Every time a patron sat down, she threw herself at them, repeating variations of, 'I need a new wife. Fuck Olivia.' Which was fine until my tips reflected otherwise. She started to literally cry and ask if she could buy a wife for two weeks." She scoffs. "All I know is that I'm never giving my future child that name. She ruined it."

"I hope there was a good reason for someone to shoot their shot at a bar less than a quarter mile from a couple's resort." I shake my head. *People be peopling.* Those with money always find a way to get theirs, regardless of the collateral damage. "I'm exhausted for you. Unfortunately, nothing surprises me anymore. Probably trying to make her ex jealous."

"Who knows? Between the constant partying on the east side and the hopeless romance on this side, most people get along around here, despite the number that have dated each other. To be fair, I've never understood the 'friends with your ex' thing. Tried it. Never again. Once I'm done, I'm *done.*"

If only I could shake off the sting of rejection from B.H.J —presumably her initials. This is why I don't do serious relationships—she wasn't even an ex. I raise my glass. "Cheers to that."

"Funnily enough, she didn't hit on me. I would've considered it, given her tip alone. Doesn't help that I'm a sucker for gorgeous eyes. Oh well." She shrugs. "I've dealt with plenty worse back in Austin. I feel for whoever has to deal with that ticking emotional time bomb." The dribbles of juice on the bartop edge get wiped clean. "Anyway, that was my night."

"Oi!" a husky voice shouts from behind me. "Are the breakfast tacos ready yet?" Sounds of click-clacking from flip-flops amplify as someone approaches.

My attention shifts toward an older white butch a few inches shorter than me with tan freckled skin. Sport sunglasses rest on top of shaggy silver hair and a tropical printed shirt is loosely tucked in the front of their cargo shorts. I squint. Is that a scarf around their neck? *Here?* We lock eyes briefly, then I casually turn to face the bar mirror.

"Make it two plates, Akari," the person adds.

I barely hold back my grimace when sensing the weight of another human plopping down beside me. *Out of all the empty seats, you just* had *to pick that one.*

"Coming right up, Lynn." Akari's warm smile and friendly wink in my direction tell me I'm in decent company, but I always question the premise.

A moment later, she sets a plate of three tacos smothered in a green sauce in front of me. The smell of smoked meat is impossible for my stomach to ignore. Anyway, I'd never refuse a kind gesture involving food. I thank Lynn with an appreciative nod, offer to buy her a drink, and start eating. Before we can engage in small talk, the bartender's eyes grow wide, and her nose scrunches as if she's talking to a baby. "Is that my favorite customer!?"

With compressed lips, I glance around for someone else and follow her line of sight. Was she talking to the scarf around Lynn's neck? When Lynn gently lifts the fleece mate-rial, a small, round body covered with brown-and-white quills pokes out, then an itty bitty nose curiously wiggles beneath its prickly exterior before ducking back inside. It's strange, but cute. I scoot my plate an inch away.

"The weather's not too hot today, so I thought I'd bring Quilliam by to say hi before we head to the office. He sleeps, mostly." Lynn directs her attention to my slack expression. "I used to help run the largest domesticated hedgehog rescue back in London. You can take an employee out of the rescue, but you can't take the rescue out of an employee. Don't worry. Quilliam is the world's happiest hedgehog."

"Right." Diverting from my chatty neighbors, I locate my phone to send Kaydence a text, but the message fails. I search for a Wi-Fi connection. Nothing.

A voice grabs my attention. "Lynn, I was telling my new friend here, uh—"

I slide the device into my pocket. "Caroline."

"Caroline—about the time I attempted to stay friends with an ex after a mutual breakup." Bartender Akari hands Lynn a mimosa. "We even did the roommate thing. One day I realized I respected her cat more than her. Apparently, so did the new girlfriend she left me for." She huffs. "I love hearing relationship drama. When it's not mine."

Lynn booms a laugh. "Sunny won't shut up about you, and I've heard this story three times now. Clearly you two miss each other." Then she points a toothy grin my way. "Don't listen to sassy-ass Akari over here. Her ex works at my resort, so she secretly hopes I'll fire her. I married mine. Mae and I have been together for so many years, I stopped counting. Another ex and I have a beautiful friendship. Then there are people I wouldn't trust a pet rock with, let alone Quilliam. Point is, your mileage may vary—"

"Correction. That killjoy misses me, *not* the other way around."

"Whatever you say." Lynn gives her a look.

Drifting into the background while they continue, I notice the silver-and-rose-gold jewelry dangling from Akari's right wrist. Lynn catches me, and she points at Akari's arm.

"Isn't that the charm bracelet Sunny gave you?" Hearing Lynn's contagious giggle makes me crack a smile. It's obvious someone is lying to themselves. This is prime-time entertainment.

Akari counters despite the hint of blush in her cheeks. "I'm hoping that Caroline's single, because I'm on the market if interested." Akari playfully winks at me. "Just say the word and I'll cancel my shift and tell the boss about my hot date tonight. I'll make sure to add that we aren't going to bed anytime soon."

I glance at the lotus flower tattoo between her breasts,

then meet her gaze. An opening to flirt. Just what I don't need—more baggage.

All eyes are on me. This is one of my favorite parts of the job. More times than not, I'm just myself rather than creating a PI persona. No one ever seems to believe me when I tell the truth.

"What if I told you I was single and a private investigator looking for a woman staying at the couples' resort? And right about now, I wish she was you." For my case's sake.

They stare at me in silence for a beat, then there's a fit of laughter from both of them. "That's a good one." Lynn says, patting me on the back. "Where *is* your partner?"

Like clockwork. I *am* staying at the resort—Kaydence said it was the only option available. I guess I should play the part. The bartender's story comes to mind. "My wife and I are here celebrating. My poor little lightweight had one too many shots last night. Can't recover like we used to." Subject change. "So, what do you do for Goddess Lagoon?"

The conversation halts when Lynn's phone illuminates the bartop. "Sorry. Mae must be finished at the spa."

A minute later, Lynn ends the call and invites my non-existent wife and I to dinner at the hibachi restaurant sometime. She gives me a rundown on the types of food on the island. There's restaurants with various cuisines dedicated to them spread throughout Sapphire Isle. Most of the food on the west side, including the resort, has Asian dishes to enjoy. She rattles off a long list of Asian countries from the east and southeast, but I can't keep up. I just ate, yet I'm already hungry again listening to her winded explanation of menu options. As friendly as she is, I want Wi-Fi, not a double date.

"Well, if you ever want to try this place and need someone to go with, my wife and I would love to have you."

A viable excuse comes to mind. "We would love to, but the lady has a long list of allergies, so stuff like sushi is a no-go. We're one of those annoying couples who are best friends that rarely stay separate for long." I flash a convincing smile. "Love and all that."

"When you meet The One, it's easy to be that way, you know?" Lynn rises to her feet and flings an arm over my shoulders like we've been friends for years, careful to not disrupt the little one. "Make sure to tell her that the restaurant has the best food I've ever tasted. And they don't just serve sushi. They have all kinds of dishes. You know, it's one of those places with the flat grills where the chefs do the fiery volcano thingy with the onions." Lynn's eyes light up in a way only a fellow foodie would understand. "That's my favorite part. Promise me you'll at least tell her. It will be fun."

The persistence is amusing. She reminds me of Mamma —an over-the-top extrovert, people person—"talk to trees to see-how-they're growing" type. Too trusting. Opposite of me. "I'll tell her, but no promises. I will say, though, I too love the fiery volcano."

"How about this…" Lynn rummages through her pockets and grumbles when she comes up empty. She quickly scans the bar and reaches for a napkin and pen. "If you change your mind, give me a call."

We wave goodbye, and I watch Lynn walk down the beach. Once she and Akari are out of sight, I crumple the paper without a glance and toss the wadded ball onto the bartop. So far, everyone seems perfectly nice, but there's no point in making friends. I'm here for work, not play.

I exit the bar, on the hunt for an internet signal. I walk toward the resort. It's about time I start on this, in Kaydence's words, "straightforward" surveillance case. No more surprises.

CHAPTER 5

BASIL

SITTING on the edge of the villa bed, I bask in a pool of my own misery. It's almost noon. Even while vacationing, I had always been an early riser. Not today. It's like my life repertoire ran away, right along with my fiancée. After failing last night's Mission Impossible: Temporary Wife Edition, it'll be at least five years until another mojito touches my lips. Sips of water help wash away the stale rum that coats my throat, but not the shame. I'm never setting foot in that bar again.

Is this what the verge of rock bottom looks like? Mojitos clearly aren't a solution to my problem. A wife is. The churning sensation canvassing my stomach confirms my decision. How am I going to maneuver past the resort's ridiculous policy? Should I give up?

My phone, resting underneath the pillow next to me—Olivia's side—vibrates, and I untangle it from the sheets. When the screen brightens, Seattle's chaos returns. Sixty-three missed calls. Fourteen voice messages. I scroll down and groan. One hundred and nine new text messages. Nothing from Olivia. She better not have the audacity.

Mother called twice. Most of the messages are from Hazel and Riley in our group chat. Mostly Hazel.

I hear the video chat chime and, against my better judgment, I answer.

"I cannot believe you still went on your honeymoon." Hazel's voice is trembling; beads of sweat linger on her forehead. Why does she look like the one who got left at the altar? "How about if you come home right now, Finn and I won't *kill* you? Riley's here to back me up." The screen shifts to Riley leaning against the kitchen countertop, looking flawless per usual, appearing light years calmer and more put together than me and Hazel combined. Her bright-yellow sundress pops nicely against her deep-mahogany skin tone. Meanwhile, I look like a bus ran me over, and my sister is ridiculous in her army-green T-shirt with ripped sleeves, shorts, and a pair of exercise gloves. Scrubs suit her better. It feels like years have gone by, not days, since the wedding. Seeing familiar faces relaxes me.

"I'm *fine*," I insist and pace around the room. "The only reason I answered your call is because your twin energy is vice-gripping my spine."

"Sorry for being a concerned sister?" Our pouting faces are identical. "Tell me what's going on."

After I inform her and Riley of my current situation, Hazel drops down on her rowing machine seat. "I don't understand. Why lie? Leaving someone at the altar says more about the other person, not you. Why don't you reschedule with the Blakemans?"

Easy for her to say. She's the only sibling that doesn't work for the family business. "*Because* I've already rescheduled twice. We can't afford to miss this deal. I'm *this* close. I can fix this."

"God, you sound like Mom. Nothing needs to be fixed. Our family name is cursed!" Hazel growls in frustration and tosses the phone. "Babe, *please* talk some sense into her."

Now, I'm looking at Riley's face. Distinct whooshing sounds increase in the background.

"I don't know why you don't listen to your sister!" she yells. Immediately, I identify Riley's fake tone. The slight upward curl in her lips is another sign. We might not talk regularly or have a typical best friendship, but we've stood by each other since we were kids. A judgment-free zone. Seconds later, her voice lowers. "Hazel has been on that rowing machine nonstop since the wedding, and I'm genuinely concerned she's going to snap. Seeing her lose her shit might be worth an early flight home."

A hollow laugh escapes my mouth. Hazel is supposed to be the calm twin. "She wouldn't hurt a fly. Worst case, she'll return to being a recluse in the forest."

"Don't tell me that. I just got her back and don't want to lose her again."

Riley's slight frown reminds me of the reason why Hazel retreated to a cabin in the woods in the first place. Heartbreak. Humiliation in front of hundreds of people, and there I was blaming her for dating a wannabe Victoria Secret model in the first place. Maybe our family name is cursed after all.

"At least she's hot as hell when she's all worked up like this." Riley's words grab my attention. "Last night, she tied me up for the first time and—"

"Oh my god. Stop!" I cut her off. The downside of your sister and childhood friend dating.

"Sorry. Forgot." She clears her throat. "One second, please. I told Hazel I'd yell at you."

She slams the sliding door on her way outside. "You're such a selfish bitch!"

My brow slants upward. *Seriously?* Brava on the acting.

The phone screen rotates, and her voice returns to her normal soothing tone. "How are you, really?"

I think for a moment, taking in the view of the crowded beach. "Honestly, I don't know. But I need this deal locked in." A win. That's what I need. My voice shakes. "I have to do this, Riley. I—"

"No explanation required. I'm here to support the mission. If I were in your shoes, I'd be doing the same thing. I'll handle Hazel. She's going through it, but she'll be fine."

"Leaving now would be more of a pain in the ass than staying. I'll devise a plan soon."

"Of course you will; you're a Jones. While you're away from all this noise, think about what *you* want in life, and when you come home, we'll be here to help. Take all the time you need. Your fancy wine business isn't going anywhere."

I dispel a breath. Something shiny catches my eye, and I halt at the foot of the bed. "Olivia will regret leaving me when she hears about my success. I don't need anyone."

There's a stretch of silence between us. I peer down at the kissing swan display resting on the bamboo bench. Around it sits shimmering embroidered lettering outlined in gold: *Welcome, Mrs. and Mrs. Jones.* Option three. Setting up our honeymoon package feels like it was yesterday, not fifteen months ago. The display is more stunning than the brochure photo, and back then, I was certain Olivia would've adored them. Back when she appreciated my intrinsic efforts. Something that had transformed into exasperated sighs and petty bickering over the years. She had never seemed to understand how I only wanted us to have a successful marriage, unlike my parents'. If only I had listened more, if only I had moved a few meetings here and there, maybe Olivia and I would still be together—no. I clench one of the swan beaks in my fist and drop it on the floor. She didn't love me enough to care about our future—our legacy—as much as I did. That's on her.

Remembering I'm on the phone, I check the screen, and Riley meets my watery gaze. "Oh, Basil, I wish I could hug you."

I fight the sob in my throat, and my voice goes soft. "Me too."

* * *

A shower and a short nap later, I reach a conclusion. I'll go to the front desk and tell them about my wife's canceled flight and see if they'll accept an electronic signature. That's when Riley will step in if need be. That will hopefully buy me time. My phone buzzes again. I peek at the screen, and my heart jolts at the name. *Oh no*. And I thought I was sick before.

"Mrs. Blakeman? Hello—hi."

"I'm glad you answered, dear." There's a notable sternness in her voice beneath the faint Thai accent I remember. "I didn't see a response to my email. That reservation works for you two, then?"

I swallow. "Uh, yes." The death grip on my phone tightens against my face as I glance around for my laptop. Wait. What did I agree to? Why the hell didn't I check my email first? My cheeks tingle from flames of deception. "We were discussing lunch plans."

"Perfect timing. How about an impromptu round of appetizers downstairs? Join us. Our treat."

"Oh, we'd hate to intrude."

"No trouble at all. We've been eager to share big news with you all week. Once inside the restaurant, hang a right, then take the stairs. You won't miss us. We cannot wait to finally meet the other Mrs. Jones that your mother has been raving about. Talk soon." The call disconnects.

My mind scrambles. Declining isn't an option, but neither is showing up with a wife. I'm quick on my feet; I wouldn't be one of Seattle's top saleswomen if I wasn't.

Downstairs, I scan the front desk as I sneak past. Thank the sapphic gods. No sign of the not-so-sunny Sunny. My mood perks, and I adjust the flounce sleeves of my dress as I enter the restaurant. Recalling Mrs. Blakeman's instructions, I pace past the tropical plants canvassing the room. Vibrant hues of fuchsia, sunburst orange, and crimson flowers paint the path forward. The restaurant shares the same aspects as the lobby—the calming aura, the spotless white marble floors and scents of fresh fruits.

I shiver at a chill in the air as I descend toward the bottom floor entering the immaculate underwater portion of the resturant. The water level rises along the gigantic wall-sized windows until it ends at the perfect angle, facing divine, crystal-blue water. Schools of fish swim through the vibrant coral reefs inside the aquarium tunnel. *Dreamy*, *romantic*, and *magnificent* are understatements. I can only imagine the glorious sight during a sunrise breakfast. Without Olivia.

I slow my footsteps to a halt and stare in awe, imagining snorkeling alongside the Pacific wildlife as if I'm inside a kaleidoscope of joyous childhood memories. When I reach the last step, barreling laughter sounds to my left. I glance over my shoulder and groan. Not again. Sunny, who appears to be finishing a tour, just excused herself and is walking in my direction.

Charged with panic, I whip around, my arm crashing into a server holding a tray chock-full of colorful cocktails. In slow motion, a streak of blood-orange liquid paints the center of my dress. Thai words I don't understand but can imagine strike the large room more loudly than the shattering glass, gasps, and clanking silverware combined.

Posthaste, I excuse myself and jolt out of sight. Not sticking around to assess the damage, I turn the corner and enter a section with significantly fewer people—and places to run. Heart drumming against my chest and not knowing the exact moment my life transformed from an epic romance to a Tarantino film, I frantically search for the Blakemans. I halt, squeezing my sides to catch my breath, and think logically. They can't see me like this. And what if Sunny approaches the table exigently demanding pen on paper?

I grab a pile of napkins and kickstart my prefrontal cortex, searching it for answers while I aggressively dab at my chest. Refusal to give any human the satisfaction of booting me off this island fuels me to locate a closet or long tablecloth to hide underneath. Seconds later, I spot a more suitable solution: a woman sitting facing the window. *Alone.* A solution that doesn't include me being marked with scents of ginger, citrus, and shame while I hide like a child inside a coat rack.

After wiping the sweat teasing my brow, I check the stain again, which seems to have tripled in size. Nothing has gone as planned, and now, a complete stranger stands as my potential savior. I growl in frustration, flinging the pile of napkins onto the table. *Look alive, Basil.* With flared nostrils, I blow the frizzy flyaway hairs out of my face, smooth my ruined dress, and march toward the table.

Whisking past the woman from behind, I yank the open chair back and drop down, two hands slapping the table with a pronounced smack. "Listen. I don't know you. You don't know me. But I need you to be my wife—"

What the hell?

"Caroline?"

She startles, the insanely attractive Caroline that I ghosted. Her eyebrows knit together, and her decadently full lips part as she studies me with the deepest brown eyes I've seen since I left her at that hotel room. I trail the contours of her perfectly muscular shoulders underneath a tank top that I've never been so jealous of. Time stills as I lose myself in a world much better than the current one. Speechless, we stare until the heat in my cheeks scorches, causing me to blink. Right as I remember how to speak, Sunny wanders into the room, approaching the table with a smug grin on her face.

Oh no.

CHAPTER 6

CAROLINE

"B.H.J?" It takes me a minute to realize it's actually her.

Her head yanks back. "What's a B.H.J?"

"Nothing. Never mind." I shake my head. "What are you doing here?" I point at her chest. "There's a little something on your dress."

After glancing behind me, she holds up her palms, whispering, "I'll do the talking."

She grabs my maroon jacket resting on top of my bag and slides into it, not bothering to roll up the oversized sleeves. The way she sinks into the chair tells me the staff member is no longer there.

"She turned around." She takes an audible breath and our eyes meet. "Me? Why are *you* here?"

"Can I—" Ignoring my question, she examines my hand without touching me. "You're not wearing a ring? Good. So you're here alone?"

It's my turn to yank my head back. "Is it difficult to say, 'Hi, I think you're the most beautiful woman I've ever seen. I'd love to buy you coffee sometime?' It's much better than your approach."

"We already tried that. Remember how the other morning turned out?" She tilts her head, that cute right dimple on full display.

"*Wow*." I scoff a laugh, recalling the spill on her clothes, ignoring the fabric's tightness around her breasts. "Says the person who looks like she lost a battle with a blender. You have some nerve to bark demands. And you know what else? I bought you breakfast. I *never* buy anyone breakfast, B.H—damn it, what's your name, anyway?"

Before I get my answer, she bolts to her feet, peering behind me. "Mrs. Blakeman?"

I twist in my chair, my gaze finding a slender Asian woman with shoulder-length hair, wearing a red maxi dress and heels that match the charcoal belt around her waist.

"We thought you got lost, Basil, dear." The woman's tone is as assertive as her body language. "I requested that Sunny keep an eye out for you. I would've called, but we had to handle a situation in the main hall. Some insidious trout destroyed two sets of pearl curtains and a patron's outfit. A sticky mess and no perpetrator in sight to skewer. Of course it was during the one time our security cameras went down."

Basil? That's a beautiful name. I watch Basil suck both lips into her mouth and smile, then tighten my jacket around herself. That explains a lot. My phone vibrates in my pocket.

Without another word, I rise from my seat, fighting to avoid Basil's burning glare as I pass. Ditching her seems cruel, yet people-pleasing isn't my top strength either. Can't argue with karma biting someone's ass. I'll pick up a dirty chai latte in her honor from next door. Steps from the doorway, I hear my name and look up.

Lynn?

The energetic butch from the bar barrels forward, arms wide open with a childlike excitement. Why is she like this?

"Twice in one day, huh?"

I retract my steps with a nervous smile and wave until I'm standing with Basil and Mae. On second thought, Basil doesn't seem so bad now.

Lynn snorts a laugh and rushes over. "Wait a minute." Her sandals clack as she approaches with an exaggerated jaw-slacked expression and pauses next to the woman in the red dress. Her finger wags in my direction, then Basil's. "Basil Jones—as in the VP of sales for Elixir Wines—is your wife?"

"Actually, we're not—"

Roaring laughter cuts me off.

Lynn looks left, and *that* Mrs. Blakeman must be her wife. "Mae, this is the woman I was telling you about. Caroline." Another side hug. "Hot damn. It's a small world, or should I say, island." Her teasing grin shifts to Basil. "By the way, you look great for the rough night you had. I hope you're feeling better."

In an instant, the room's temperature skyrockets. My mind races for respectful ways to get Lynn to shut the hell up; meanwhile, Basil's skin blooms a shade of red I didn't know existed.

"It's great to finally meet both of you in person," Basil says awkwardly, blush still evident in her cheeks.

"Let me tell you about the time we went to Amsterdam—"

"Stay on track, love. The appetizers are getting cold." Mae flashes her wife a thin smile and grabs her hand. "Shall we? Our table's this way." She and Lynn start walking ahead.

We shall not, I want to say, then I feel a gentle hand on my back. I turn my head and meet Basil's blue eyes. They're beautiful. We don't exchange words, instead I nod in agreement, giving into them, just like I did back in Seattle.

Inside the other room of the restaurant, we sit at the Blakemans' table. The food looks incredible. I'm not here to eat a meal I didn't plan for, but the smell of roasted garlic and lemon from the shrimp makes my mouth water. I can't help myself and join the others eating.

"Sunny will be here any second," Mae says across from Basil and I. "So why don't you tell the Joneses the delightful news? We have thirteen minutes until our meeting with the Tier One members."

I pray that this nightmare doesn't get any worse.

"Raaaat!" The scream is loud enough that heads across the room turn. "There's a fucking rodent on your pants!" Eyes wide with terror, Basil chucks my jacket at Lynn's crotch. Thankfully, her aim is awful. "It's a mutated porcupine rat. They'll multiply. We have to burn this place down. Now!"

"That's a hedgehog, dear," Mae calmly states amidst Basil's meltdown. "His middle name is Compromise. *Marriage* compromise. You know the rules, love. No hogs at the table."

Lynn shields herself from Basil a seat over. "Quilliam just wanted to say hi…"

"*Not* at the table." Mae gives a stern look.

Basil cringes and populates dramatic choking motions as Lynn carefully places the animal inside the shoe box–sized carrier. "Why is it foaming at the mouth?"

Lynn puts hypothetical earmuffs around the carrier. "Self-anointing isn't Quilliam's most appealing quality, but calling him a rodent is simply disrespectful. He's a member of the Erinaceidae family."

"Shouldn't someone be *calling* Wildlife Control—if burning the place down isn't an option?"

Basil, who's officially sitting on my lap in a non-sexy way, frantically searches the table for answers. "Am I the only person who sees that mutant creature right now?"

We all stare, speechless. *Please don't get any closer,* I almost say. She reeks of cocktail sauce, sweat, and stupidity. Clearly, Basil doesn't get out much. Or maybe she just discovered a new phobia.

When her stormy blue eyes meet mine for a response, defeated, I shrug. "He's the world's happiest hedgehog." I help Basil put the jacket back on to hide the stain on her dress again.

Sunny arrives minutes later. She doesn't seem a quarter as thrilled to be here as Lynn; then again, no one does. "Mrs. Blakeman, I printed out the attendance report. If I recall, the Joneses are on the list. I can run back to my desk and grab it to confirm." Sunny faces Basil and flutters her eyes, which seems ill-received based on the dagger looks they exchange. "As I told Mrs. Jones yesterday, it's *imperative* we receive all guests' signatures."

I squint at Basil. "Signatures? What's she talking about?"

Lynn waves a hand in the air. "Never mind all that. I know that everyone who's staying in a room needs a signature on file, but these two lovebirds are our special guests. Just slap my initials in the box."

Mae nods. "You might think we're being over the top, but you wouldn't believe the monsters that try to pull a fast one over the resort, especially when the east side suits are sold out. Sunny here once got to the bottom of an eight-woman polycule situation. Three women checked in, and five more showed up days later asking how to get to the Sapphire East. It's a shame when people lie and take advantage of good hospitality."

"It also ruins opportunities for those who cultivate and champion genuine, loving, real polyamorous relationships, unlike *some* people I know," Sunny says, a little too passionately.

Lynn holds up a finger with an awkward chuckle. "Let's not go down that depressing rabbit hole."

I recall the bar talk from earlier.

Lynn continues, "I have a feeling these two will end up as

leading contenders for the tournament. Finally, some real competition for the champs worth watching."

"What tournament?" Basil and I blurt out simultaneously.

Mae jumps in. "Five minutes. Get to the point, love."

"Almost there." Lynn grins. "There'll be plenty of time to discuss the Sapphic Olympics at the hibachi restaurant. We're still on for tomorrow, right?"

What? That's not the bar conversation I remember. "No—"

"Yes!" Basil shouts over me. "Two p.m."

I yank my head toward my fake wife's direction. "Let's not make any rash decisions without further discussion, *honey*."

Lynn claps her hands together and glances at her watch. "Great. Just enough time for the big news." Her eyes shimmer with excitement. "We got you a wedding gift."

"No, no, no." I shake my head in a rapid windshield-wiper motion. "We can't accept."

"A villa upgrade is the least we could do." Mae offers a genuine smile. "You're the ones who graciously rescheduled your honeymoon to offer a client relationship–building opportunity. You're a potential business partner. Even though we're the client, we'll still spoil you like proper guests."

"Did we, now?" My side-eye is deadly. "We're going to *work* on our honeymoon?"

"That is, if you don't mind some missing custom details from your original reservation," Lynn adds. "The Honey Hut Villa, gold package, is our best model. There are three units, and you two get the last one." She whips out a game-show host tone, waving both arms in the air and pausing to speak into the invisible mic. "Ocean view. Private deck and beach. Top shelf minibar. Skylight window. And my personal favorite selling point…" She leans close as if to tell us a secret and whispers, "Soundproof walls."

This cannot be happening. I blink twice. It's not like I'll use the soundproofing, outside of screaming at Kaydence for getting me into this mess. I stare at a dot on the floor, ignoring teasing elbow jabs from Lynn.

Taking a deep breath, I quit fighting and accept my fate—and the two shiny new villa keys.

Time blurs by until Basil and I are alone. This is bad. I don't have time for this debacle, especially not with the woman who ghosted me days ago.

Basil, appearing still as stunned as I am, breaks the silence. "I have so many questions. First, how are they a couple?"

Taking a hand, I massage my temples. "Better yet, how are *we* a couple? *Basil.*"

"Well…" She holds the key to eye level. "Perhaps we should further discuss our arrangement this evening."

Arrangement? I face her with arms crossed over my chest. "There is no arrangement." My jaw tightens. "And I don't need whatever you're offering."

"But you do need a place to sleep." Basil eyes me carefully. "It became painfully apparent during the conversation with the Blakemans that you were unaware of the policy. Now, excuse me, I have to get out of this dress. *All* by myself." Her eyes linger on my lips before she walks away.

It's like she knows I'm checking her out. "That line won't work on me twice," I holler, and she flashes a smile over her shoulder.

Each sway of her hips reminds me of our night together. Talking and laughing until the rest of the world drifted away, my hands resting perfectly on her waist on the dance floor. Running my lips along her neck, feeling her pulse jolt underneath my touch. The way she pleaded for me to taste her and how I refused until her lips moved exactly where I wanted them.

As she sashays away without a look back, I lick my lips and take a deep breath. I remember why I'm on this island in the first place: the case. I was just about to open Kaydence's email before I got interrupted.

In dire need of fresh air, I exit the building and sit at a table on the beach. A gentle breeze cools the heat forming between my thighs from the salacious memories overtaking my mind. Headphones on, I press Play on my running playlist and open the email. I scan the pages, and my thumb halts on a picture of two women. My eyes dart to the one posing on the left: brunette hair, warm smile, memorable right dimple. Wearing a blazer that compliments her blue irises. There's a flashy rock on her ring finger.

My eyes grow wide when I read the print below the image. My target. Basil Harper Jones.

CHAPTER 7

CAROLINE

"Excuse me, she's your what?!" Kaydence's yelp makes me yank the phone from my ear.

With my back against the wooden bridge railing leading to the villa, I let the endless starry night hovering over the ocean capture my attention while she rants. The warm air and gentle breeze calms my mind, unlike the person on the line currently. I know she's preparing to fight the idea of me playing house with my target, though admittedly at this point I don't see another option.

"You've been on Lesbo Island for five minutes and now you have a whole-ass wife? If this isn't Vegas—"

"What am I supposed to do?" I reiterate, keeping my voice low. "Besides, how is this only my fault? We both know I would have had plenty of options for outsourcing if you'd informed me about the policy."

"Okay." She exhales. "That was my bad. Sapphire East was sold out, so I went with what was available, but that doesn't translate to you going and marrying your target...Christ, King." Kaydence angrily whispers, "Make it make sense."

"Quit comparing this to a drunken night in Vegas. There

47

are no legally binding documents. The bright side is I'd be close enough where she'd expect me around. That way I won't risk her catching me tailing her. The island's big, but not that big. See? Queer Logic 101. What could go wrong?" A hunch tells me I won't have issues. Then an image of Basil's smooth legs and what I'd do between them crosses my mind. I force the thought away.

"What could go wrong?" Kaydence repeats my words, then I hear her signature maniacal laughter. "You're at one of the world's most romantic honeymoon islands, stuck married to your *target*—who happens to be a woman you already hooked up with. A million things could go wrong, Miss Captain-Save-A—" Pause. She starts over, calmer this time. "I mean, the most likely outcome is your cover gets blown and she poisons you and throws your goofy ass into the ocean. If she doesn't, maybe I will."

I should be upset, but I can't help but laugh when she gets like this. "Trust me, Jones is hot and harmless—and clueless about the case. Sure, she's grumpier than that drill sergeant who found out you slept with his wife back in the day. And I would be too if I was left at the altar like Jones. "

"*Ex*-wife," she mutters. "And quit changing the subject, King."

A stretch of silence allows me to think. I know, on top of everything else, Kaydence doesn't need another person to worry about. A pregnant wife and toddler is enough. Nikita's IVF journey this round hasn't been as successful as they'd hoped, and Kaydence tends to keep her emotions to herself at risk of not appearing to have her house in order. The last thing I want is to add to her stress. I also know our call won't end until she feels unwavering confidence in the situation.

"I'm going to do my job, that's it," I say matter-of-factly. With every ounce of reassurance I can muster, and a firm tone, I continue, "You know my rules."

"Close cases, get paid. Don't mix work with pleasure. Yeah, yeah…" A deep chuckle—the white flag I was hoping for—finally descends.

Yes, having slept with a target could put me in a compromising situation, but I've had my reputation on the line in the past, and I won't let that happen again. Lust and love be damned.

"I owe you one for dealing with this client," Kaydence says. "The money's great, but she's something else. I've had to review what PI work is and what it isn't because she asked about *wiretaps*. Jesus. Who does she think we are? FBI? My official mission is to figure out exactly *who* this woman is. Stay tuned." Rosie's cries echo in the background. "Until then, mommy time."

Our call ends, and I wait outside the villa door for my increasing heart rate to steady. Why am I nervous? I'm not the same person I was when I fell in love with a narcissist. And I don't regret sleeping with Basil in the first place, but I hope she got what she needed that night, because it's never going to happen again.

Having my own key to the honeymoon villa doesn't help me digest the fact that she hasn't left my mind since the rooftop party—or that I'm fake-married to her. Maybe showing up isn't a wise idea, but I can't deny my growing intrigue.

Never mind. I just need to finish this case and get back to the States.

Entering the foyer, I drop my bag on the entryway bench. Within seconds, I lock eyes with Basil, who's sitting in the living area with pen in hand. Papers are spread out on the coffee table. She's no longer wearing her outfit from earlier; now, it's a black dress. Heels. Makeup. Her hair is pulled up, but I can tell it isn't fully dried.

She's up to something.

And she's mistaken if she believes I'll let her outfit distract me. We exchange polite smiles and I sit down in the chair next to her.

"How do you know the owners?" she asks after handing me a tiny bottle of water from the minibar. She takes a sip of hers and swings one leg over the other.

"Lynn Blakeman seems to know you."

I note her shift in body position but maintain eye contact. "We had a brief conversation this morning at the bar. How do you know them?"

"Business." Her attention is back on the paperwork. "And apparently, now business with you. Look. I won't bore you with the details, but I wasn't aware of the resort's policy. Apparently, neither were you, and somehow the Blakemans believe you're my wife, someone that doesn't exist. Hence the dilemma."

I can't resist asking the question that's been circling my mind since I read the case file. "Were you in a relationship when we—?" I believe I know the answer, but part of me wants to hear her say it, to confirm.

She shakes her head. "I'm not a cheater. She was...probably." Her gaze points toward the floor. "And you're at a couple's resort because?"

The way she's shifting tells me she's uncomfortable. I'm not heartless, so I don't press her for details on the breakup. "Solo trip. Sapphire East was full."

She nods.

I take a deep breath. I figure I might as well commit. Plus, I remember my promise to Kaydence that I have everything under control. "Fine," I say. "What's our plan?"

For the next thirty minutes, we discuss our agreement.

"It's just for appearances, nothing more. Participation in the scheduled items should be minimal, if necessary at all. Here's your copy of the itinerary. The yellow highlights are the events. Blue highlights are locations. I added the columns, which read left to right: event start times, your arrival time, and attire. On the back are details about our relationship, such as how we met, my favorite color, allergies, dietary restrictions—"

My brows crinkle together when she hands me a stack of papers.

"Sorry, the gift shop doesn't sell binders."

"Why do I need to read this? We're not a real couple."

She doesn't seem to like my response. "No. But we need to pass as one. What if people ask you questions about me?"

"I'll make up an answer?"

"Wrong." She intertwines her fingers together and rests her hands on her knee. "I'm open to negotiation regarding the details; however, the itinerary stands."

Leaning back, I drape an arm on the couch backrest, and a corner of my mouth curls. These demands are cute. "I don't remember you being this bossy in the hotel room. *Quite* the opposite."

We hold each other's gaze. I indulge myself in a memory of her hands pinned above her head against the door, with me trapping her moans with my mouth. When her sight drifts to my lips and back up, I wonder what she's thinking.

I clear my throat. "I'll do it if you change one item." I scan for the section I'm looking for. The weight of her gaze strengthens as I strike through three lines, add my own notes, and hand the papers back. "Here."

She reads the *How We Met* section out loud. "Basil swiped right, then asked Caroline out on a date."

She scoffs. "I refuse to tell anyone, especially the Blakemans, that I *swiped* anything."

If I'm stuck married to her, I might as well make her grovel a few times. She hates that, I'm sure. "Meeting online is more believable than meeting at some stuffy business conference."

"Since when?"

"That's what I want adjusted. Think of it as a proper proposal."

Exasperation is written all over her face. "Are we seriously debating about a dating app right now?"

"Yes."

The way she fights holding back an eye roll would be adorable if she wasn't my target. She fixes her face and plasters on an obviously fake smile. Her dimple usually shows otherwise. "Of course I swiped right; otherwise, we wouldn't be a couple, now, would we, *honey*?"

"And I declined three times before accepting out of sheer pity. Luckily for us, you grew on me." A finger on my chin, I think for a moment. "For our first date, we went to a latte art class at a coffee shop." I smile. "Because I used to be a barista."

Her raised brow meets my smug grin. "Anything else?"

"And we made vanilla dirty chai lattes."

She slams her arms to her lap. "Are you enjoying yourself?"

"A little," I admit. A suppressed laugh escapes my lips. She probably thinks I'm incorrigible. "You aren't?"

"No, because this isn't a joke. We have lunch with the Blakemans tomorrow. You need to be prepared to play the part of being a Jones. While I figure out how to make up ground with Quilliam the hedgehog." She shudders in disgust.

I raise both palms into the air. "All right, all right."

Sitting across from me, she's reviewing the itinerary line by line, talking to herself and briskly switching between highlighters and pen. Oh, she's irritated, but I don't care. I won't let her get under my skin. I won't risk my job or my heart ever again.

Intently, I watch her. *Basil Harper Jones, I don't know why my client wants a tail on you, but I'm going to learn every single detail about you. You're never leaving my sight.*

After downing the rest of her water, Basil returns to the minibar and pours a healthy serving of chardonnay. This is going to be one of many long nights.

She looks up, and a smile tugs at her lips when she catches me checking her out for the third time. "Next topic: sleeping arrangements."

CHAPTER 8

BASIL

I⊤'s twenty minutes until 2 p.m. the next day. I'm waiting in the foyer while Caroline finishes getting ready so we can meet the Blakemans at the restaurant down the road. My phone vibrates in my hand. When I check the screen, I see a text message from my mother.

JULIETTE

Update?

"Hello, Mother. I'm working on it as we speak," I grumble to myself as I type my response. She's quick to get to the point, without a morsel of compassion for my situation, it seems. Always business first with Juliette Jones. Mothering second. I smash the Send button.

BASIL

Lunch meeting with the Blakemans in 15.

I understand the circumstances aren't ideal, but a positive impression is imperative. I'm counting on you.

I huff. *Not ideal? Not ideal?!* Was she at the same wedding I was? I hammer my fingers against the phone keyboard.

> Did you forget that I'm a Jones? I will see this deal to the finish line. There are obstacles, but I am working through them.

What obstacles?

> Nothing I can't handle.

As long as we get results. Even if that means patching things up with Olivia. I've mitigated the situation, but you need to do your part.

What does that mean, exactly? Mitigated how? My grip tightens around my phone. Simply *reading* Olivia's name knots my stomach. I hover a finger over my mother's name to initiate a phone call, then remember my "obstacle" within earshot distance and change my mind.

> I always do.

I want meeting details later.

> Yes, ma'am.

Look alive, Basil.

I don't bother responding and put the phone away when the bathroom door opens as Caroline exits. My exasperation with my mother subsides with each second I fight the urge to gawk at the woman in front of me. Caroline looks damn good in that pink-and-white-striped button-down shirt. Cuffed dark jeans, sunglasses in one hand. Brown coils of hair pop under her tan, wide-brimmed fedora hat. I take in her tall frame, which seems to tower over me all of a sudden. Her crisp sleeves hug the swell of her biceps just right. Her outfit complements the navy accents of my sundress, as if she had me in mind when making her outfit decision. I meet her bright, toothy grin. God, her smile is beautiful. She knows I approve.

Unable to help myself, the corners of my lips curl upward. "You clean up well."

"I try on occasion. You look nice." It's not the first time she's seen my outfit today, but you couldn't tell based on how she's looking at me. Nonetheless, I'll take the compliment.

"Thank you." I turn to hide the heat traveling to my cheeks and grab the doorknob, but pause, sensing Caroline's weighted gaze on my backside. "Ready?"

The sounds of her footsteps close in, pinning me to the spot. My heartbeat quickens at how close she is. The clean scent of her perfume fills my nose, reminding me of a picture-perfect day on the water. Fruity, aquatic notes; ravishing woody finish. She looks like a dreamboat and smells like one too.

"I'm ready for sweet *and* spicy Basil today."

I sandwich my bottom lip between my teeth and toss a smile over my shoulder. "Your herb jokes still aren't funny." I step back, creating space to open the door. "Remember, you're a Jones now. Look alive."

As we pass through the lobby, I snicker at the giant floor sign near the front desk. *All party signatures are required upon check-in.* I wonder how many people will experience the wrath of the raging Sunny this week. At least I'm clear of that shitshow.

A familiar voice ahead makes me halt. A woman standing near the resort entrance makes eye contact with me. I know her. My eyes narrow into slits, and my muscles tense. *No.*

As if my life couldn't get any worse.

Victoria fucking Miller is here. I plaster a fake smile at my high-school—is there a stronger word for *nemesis*? I expel a breath. That was a long time ago. Jones women are above petty behavior toward others. Usually. But, this snake is an exception.

"Do I know—*oh*, Victoria. I almost didn't recognize you. Nice to see you...here." I study her pixie hairstyle, a deeper red than I remember. She's wearing thick rimmed glasses that practically cover her face, a dress as orange as her skin, and a purse dangling from the crook of her elbow. The only thing missing is the teacup Pomeranian.

"What's it been? Half a decade?" Her nails-on-a-chalk-board voice is one thing that hasn't changed over the years. "I was hoping to bump into you sooner than later. We heard you would be here." She flaunts a smile like she'd one-upped me, and I tilt my head in confusion. "We're practically VIP and privy to insider information."

She introduces Caroline and me to her wife, Lauren, standing next to her. A fit woman with strong cheekbones and fair skin. Wait a damn minute. Victoria Miller. Not straight? And OUT? The same person who declared all senior year that my sister was stalking her when a teacher caught them kissing? Quite the paradox.

Victoria eyes Caroline down then up. "Hi. Are you Basil's assistant or—?"

"*Vicky.*" I know she hates being called that. "My wife and I are enjoying our honeymoon. The gold package...with the soundproof walls."

"Noted. So are we. We've been coming here for years. It's unfortunate when prestigious vacation islands start opening up to the general public." Victoria's grin turns cunning. "Excuse us. We girl-bossed too hard at the beach and need to rest. Let's go, baby."

Lauren—Barbie's sister—appears to be just as dumbfounded as Caroline. I glare at the back of her head until they're out of sight. I couldn't stand Victoria Miller when we were kids, and seeing her again reminds me how much I still loathe her presence. Sure, grudges are petty, but that was my twin sister she hurt. I'll never forget Hazel's tears the day she told me what happened or her hopelessness as the rumor mill churned in the months following. I'm convinced every villain origin story starts with Victoria.

Under different circumstances, I would have reminded— more like *buried*—Vicky with accolades Hazel and I have gained over the last decade, jogging her memory and warning her to never challenge a Jones again, but I have more important things in my life to address. She's not worth my time.

Since decking Icky Vicky in the face is frowned upon, I cross my arms over my chest and mutter louder than I intended, "We're two unashamed women doing *very* lesbian things together. Bitch."

Without another word, I march outside, disregarding Caroline's shocked expression altogether.

* * *

We don't exchange words during our short walk to the hibachi restaurant. I have no clue how to recover from my "Doing very lesbian things" line. Plus, I despise small talk as much as I do meetings that should've been an email. I shift my focus away from Caroline—who occupied my mind all night—and bask in the island's festivities. I adjust my sunhat to shield my eyes from the rays as I peer down the shore. An intense beach volleyball game is in progress. The ball bounces back and forth over the net until someone spikes it and scores. Cheers and high fives get passed around. Further down, several women are lazily suntanning, a task I'm looking forward to.

When we reach our destination, Caroline pauses in front of the entrance doors. "Mind telling me what that was about back there?"

"I do mind."

"Okay…" She pulls the door open. "Let's go do one of my favorite 'very lesbian things': eating. After you." As I pass through the entrance, she adds, "And if anyone asks, you have a seaweed allergy."

My arms drop in exasperation. "If you actually read the itinerary, you would've known that I love spicy tuna rolls. Now, you're telling me I can't—you know what? Never mind." I end my rant and walk inside.

When we reach our table in the dim back corner, Lynn, the more animated of the Blakemans, tackles Caroline into a hug before shaking my hand. Why don't I get that type of reaction? I'm huggable, aren't I? I take Mae's outstretched hand and firmly shake it. Being able to elicit a subtle smile from her makes me forget about the effortless relationship between my fake wife and Lynn. Once we're seated around the flat-top grill, the waitress takes our drink orders and disappears to the back.

For the last few months, I've mostly interacted with Mae. Now, I'm putting as much distance as possible between Caroline and Lynn, hoping they won't get *too* chatty, as my mission requires this meeting to go smoothly. The last thing I need is us fumbling over relationship details. Caroline comments about the number of women chefs, and Lynn tells us this is the only women-owned, women-run hibachi restaurant in the world. Caroline and I exchange satisfied smiles, appreciating the multitude of awards the establishment has achieved.

Just as I open my mouth to speak, Lynn asks what

everyone is ordering and pulls her glasses from her shirt pocket—her quirky, but somehow-manages-to-work-for-her black button-down shirt covered with tiny tacos.

"I think I'll try something new today," Lynn says, putting down her napkin on her lap. "Perhaps the salmon."

"You say that every time, love," Mae chimes in.

"Today is the day."

Mae chuckles, then leans over to me, whispering, "Watch, she'll get the shrimp yaki noodles and the lamb lollipop appetizer. If you can convince her otherwise, I'll give you an insider tip on our next project. One that requires *three times* more wine."

I cough. Did I hear that right? The expression on Mae's face tells me she's deadly serious. This is the type of information—leverage—I need to obtain. I straighten my back and watch Lynn close the menu with a content smile.

"You're on," I challenge her daring lipstick grin. I know it's a test, one I intend to win. This reminds me of the time I watched a man bet my mother a patch of land over a round of golf. I was sixteen and into my fourth year of golf lessons. I had a love-hate relationship with the sport, because although competing and winning against Victoria Miller in school never got old, accompanying my mother on business trips did. I'll never forget her smile as she handed me the club to play in her place. After my victory, on the way home, she told me, "Confucius said, 'Never give a sword to a man who can't dance.' Well, I say, give it to a woman." A rare mother-daughter moment. That day, I made a vow to sustain a Jones level of power and confidence. On my eighteenth birthday, she gifted me the land. All these years later and it's still sitting stagnant in California for no reason except principle.

Lynn's words snaps me back to the conversation. "I know,

but I've been meaning to try the choo chee salmon for a while now."

"That dish sounds fantastic, Mrs. Blakeman." I poke my head forward. "I'll join you in ordering that. We can compare notes." I despise curry, but everyone has a price.

"Absolutely." Lynn nods. "This is what breaking bread is all about. Unity and creating new experiences together."

Caroline's arm keeps brushing against mine, probably because we're crammed into the corner seats, or at least that's what I'll keep telling myself. Recalling that we're a couple on our honeymoon, I let myself lean closer and melt into her warmth. I can't determine her facial expression when she glances toward me. I offer a quick smile, hoping she plays the part. Hesitantly, she lifts her arm and rests it on the back of my chair.

"In fact." I inch a little closer and continue, "Caroline was just talking about her salmon craving. She gets on these incredible food kicks and will eat the same dish in a variety of ways for weeks." She doesn't catch on until I tap the menu.

Her brow crinkles, and she purses her lips. "Actually, I was thinking about ordering the lamb."

I flash her a sharp look, muttering, "But I bet the salmon is to *die* for."

Our gaze holds. Message received. A smile splits her lips, and her arm wraps more tightly around my shoulders as she addresses the table. "Her love is so abundant. Gripping, even."

Lynn beams a wide-eyed expression. "If you like lamb, the lollipops are an amazing option."

"You know what? I think I will." Caroline peers over at Lynn, ignoring me altogether, and in seconds, I see where my luck is headed. "I've never had lamb before. After all, this is what breaking bread is all about."

"Exactly." Lynn motions her hands into the air; meanwhile, my eye twitches. The waitress returns to take our orders. "There's just *something* about that sauce…" Lynn appears in deep contemplation, now gripping the menu an inch from her face.

I order the salmon and wait, watching Lynn battle herself as if choosing an appetizer is the last decision she'll make on this planet.

"Okay, I'm ready," Lynn announces after what seems like forever. Her smile directs at the woman patiently waiting, pen and notepad in hand. "I'll have the salmon too."

Relieved, I expel the breath I'm holding. After the waitress scribbles on the notepad and collects the menus, a victorious grin forms across my lips. It widens at Mae, who simply remains facing forward, appearing unfazed.

Caroline's next question wipes the grin from my face. Of course it's about the yaki noodles. Luckily, she sticks to her original order.

"Wait," Lynn shouts just as the waitress turns. "I might as well get my usual, then. That way Caroline can try some of mine. That's two new experiences for the price of one. I'll order the salmon next time."

I feel the weight of Mae's grin in my direction. She finds my ear. "If you want to partner with us, a piece of advice, dear." She elegantly folds her hands together. "I'm always right. And pandering will get you nowhere."

All I can do is return her smile. Damn it. I don't know which is worse, being stuck with Caroline or the reality that my biggest client to date seems to loathe me and *love* my pretend wife. Fifteen minutes later, the smell of red meat tickles my nose when Caroline's appetizer gets placed in front of her. I fight my grimace, watching her slice her food.

"Honey, this lamb is incredible." Caroline holds up her fork with a piece of meat, a careful hand underneath. "Try it."

The gesture is sweet enough. Or would be, if she were

literally anyone else. Or if I ate red meat. "Thank you, but I have plenty of food," I respond as my untouched plate of fish swimming in a pool of overwhelming red curry sauce mocks me.

"Just a bite." Caroline beckons until her brows scrunches in confusion and she lowers her voice. "I'm trying to be romantic here."

I force a chuckle and bask in a spotlight I'd normally enjoy. Caroline clearly hasn't read the itinerary.

"I don't deserve you," I mutter, jaw tightening at the dangling lamb hovering inches from my face. The entire table is waiting for my gullet to open.

To my relief, whooshing sounds from a large fire and cheering at the neighboring table yank Lynn and Mae's attention away, granting me an opening to slap the fork to the floor. When Caroline dips below the table, I follow.

"I'm pescatarian," I whisper angrily.

Caroline whispers, "Whoops."

My eyes grow into slits. "It was on the itinerary."

Caroline is exasperating. I fix my face, and we emerge with wide smiles, facing our lunch companions like a happy couple.

Several minutes pass, and everyone's busy eating, except me. I chalk up the meal as the price of business and stomach a few bites before Lynn or Mae can make a comment.

Caroline breaks the silence to ask the Blakemans a question. "What was your reasoning for changing from selling solar panels to owning resorts?"

"One, we truly believe there needs to be more safe spaces exclusively for queer folks—especially to feel safe and brave to be ourselves," Lynn says. "Two, once you're as involved in energy consumption as we are, saving the environment becomes a part of every decision. So we decided to start a business that incorporates the two. It's not the cheapest business model, but we do it for the cause."

"We appreciate that the owners respect the land we're on. Every business on the island is required to pay fees that go directly to the Thai community. Given I have family near here, it's appreciated because most private owners take advantage," Mae says, reaching for Lynn's hand. "It's critical for us to have partnerships with people who align with our vision. Helping Sapphire Isle's community is a necessity. Living on a beach isn't so bad, either."

My heart warms. Their emphasis on community and green practices are two of the many attractive factors for me working with them, and, of course, a queer couple dominating the industry is always glorious. I raise my glass to the center for a toast. "I know I should speak on behalf of Elixir Wines, but…" I hesitate. They're all staring at me and my raised glass. I clear my throat. "If I can just speak for myself for a second, I want you to know that I'm grateful for the opportunity to work with you," I say, a little awkwardly. "We try to only partner with people who share our values, too, but…well, I don't always get to work with people who are not only successful, but also compassionate and brilliant." I have no idea if this is coming out right. No one in my family gets this sappy, but I want the Blakemans to know what's in my heart. "Over the past day, I've gotten to see how you run things around here, and I'm impressed and honored. Watching two women in love and succeeding together in business truly is phenomenal." I hope they know I mean every word.

Relief floods over me. It's the first time I've seen Mae smile this wide.

"Thank you for your kind words," Mae says after taking a sip. "Elixir Wines isn't the only company we're looking to partner with this year. Recently, we hired a PR agency. One of our Tier One member's businesses, actually. We're growing fast, thanks to this one's networking." She motions toward her wife.

"Hell, I'm just grateful I get the opportunity to enjoy this with you all." Lynn gently squeezes Mae's fingers. "There was a time where I didn't think I would. A life-or-death experience changes how you used to live. After six surgeries and eighteen months of rehab—" Lynn faces her wife with a serious expression that I haven't seen before. "I learned an important life lesson to cherish every second with the people that set your heart on fire. So here I am, alive and happy. On this gorgeous island. With this extraordinary human."

Mae Blakeman may be known as one of the fiercest business women in the industry, but the way her fingers brush her wife's cheek, her gaze full of adoration and tenderness, hits me unexpectedly. A hollowness in my chest expands. How can I ever trust someone like that again?

The thought vanishes when a waitress serves a round of complimentary desserts.

"Lynn makes it difficult to not smile, doesn't she?" Mae's eyes glisten with emotion as she pecks her wife's lips. "As cliché as it sounds, life really is too short…if you let it be. For us, love wins everyday. Together for thirty-three years, married for ten. We're celebrating our anniversary soon."

Lynn's eyes grow into a childlike expression of glee, which annoys me less now than it would have earlier in the night. "You two should join. It's next week at the Gala. We'll save you seats at our table." She chuckles. "Don't worry, we'll eat well. I have an in with the chef."

A flash of heat travels to my cheeks at the thought of being in such a formal setting with Caroline. I already struggle to not gawk at her.

Mae looks at Lynn. "Some days, I wish your nose was as invested in our inventory tracking as it is in the chef's menu choices. If you don't leave that woman alone, I'm concerned she's going to quit." She faces Caroline and me, motioning a hand to the air. "I keep telling her, just because she *can* eat garlic shrimp every single day doesn't mean the entire island likes greasy, buttery, breath-stinking shrimp."

We laugh. Apparently, opposites do attract. Watching the two, I wouldn't have thought they'd ever spoken to one another before, let alone been business partners and happily together for three decades. Lynn brings out Mae's playful side, even if only for brief moments. My gaze drifts toward the tabletop. I guess I never believed having someone complement me in a relationship was good. I thought that meant I wasn't living up to my fullest potential by relying on someone. Clearly these two make it work. Why couldn't I?

Lynn's wide smile in my direction snaps me out of my dejected mood. "I have to ask, being at a couple's resort and all. How'd you two lovebirds meet? And don't let Mae's icy resolve fool you. She *loves* the cheesy stuff." Lynn meets her wife's playful eye roll.

Caroline's slack-jawed expression finds me and she faces the table. Her guilty face screams she hasn't read the itinerary and that I need to take over.

"We met at a business conference. Love at first sight." I paint a convincing smile on my lips and pat the top of her thigh underneath the table. She doesn't move away. "I won't hold it against you for not remembering what I was wearing the first day we met."

Our eyes hold, then the heat of her skin vanishes from my fingertips and she responds, "How could I forget that perfect sight?" She pauses and takes a large gulp of her drink. There's that devious grin again. "Basil went to the wrong hotel room...*my* room. I somehow didn't close the door all the way on my way out to a workshop. She made herself right at home, took a shower and everything, because when I walked in, she was butt nak—"

"She's joking," I blurt out. "We met online. Nothing special." Given Caroline's smirk, she seems quite amused with herself. "Perhaps a career in comedy would've suited her."

"There's nothing wrong with meeting online, dear," Mae says.

"Not at all." Lynn nods in agreement. "However you find your life partner—" They exchange loving smiles. "It's all special."

An hour later, dinner is over. We barely survived. This will be the last time I deal with Caroline. Now that the Blakemans have officially met my wife, I'll say she came down with an illness. Anything but another double date. Outside of sleeping under the same roof, we are no longer required to speak. The more I think about Caroline, the more I look forward to sunbathing and getting back to my book girlfriend. *She* would have read the itinerary. We exit the restaurant, passing the fish pond beneath the wooden bridge.

Lynn reminds us that each gold-member team receives a bye—automatically advances to the next round—for the Sapphic Olympics Tournament. "We'll be rooting for you on the sidelines. And will celebrate your victory *and* our anniversary at the Gala."

Great. So much for my plans of not engaging with Caroline. I attempt to curb any expectations of Caroline and I's togetherness. I smile, but Lynn seems to sense my reluctance. "We'll be there, pending any injuries—"

"Oh, come on. You two have to come up for air every once in a while...Unless she's *that* good." Lynn winks at me and then Caroline, who barely suppresses a laugh; meanwhile, my cheeks ignite involuntarily.

"I meant—"

Mae chimes in. "What my wife is attempting to say is that you two have been such lovely company. We take pride in having our business partners celebrate with us for special occasions. This is one of those occasions, and this is your official invitation. Heavy hors d'oeuvres, bottle service, burlesque performance, dance floor, all that."

"I'm not much for dancing," Caroline says. Clearly that's not the case, given how handsy we were on that rooftop.

Mae blinks. Her serious face is back. "And proceeds go to charity." She intertwines her fingers with Lynn's.

"*Exactly.* So you'll be there?" Lynn begins to walk away, then pauses, tilts her head back, and cautiously eyes me and Caroline. "Yes?"

"Wouldn't miss it for the world." I plaster on a grin. I'm tempted to look over at Caroline but don't. Thankfully, she doesn't object.

"Perfect, dear." Mae's business tone is back. "Make sure to mind your attendance. The Gala requires ninety percent for entry since we want those who make the most of their experience to be invited. Sunny oversees the roll-call data."

They wave goodbye and stroll away. Once they're out of sight, my face scrunches with discontent. The afternoon heat isn't helping subside my irritation. Despite the itinerary, I hadn't planned to complete *one* percent of the couple events with Caroline, let alone ninety, but now it looks like we don't have a choice. I'm not missing that Gala.

In front of me, Caroline shoves her hands in her pockets and has the audacity to wear that shit-eating grin on her face. "I think that went pretty well. Much better than our first date."

"Really, you think?" My glare points her direction. "Just read the damn itinerary. We have our first event tomorrow morning." Without a glance back, I march past my fake wife and head toward the villa.

CHAPTER 9

CAROLINE

"I DON'T WANT to go to couples' therapy," I tell Basil for the third time, a conviction in my voice that surprises even me this early in the morning. My stomach growls. Skipping breakfast was a terrible decision.

Basil faces me, arms crossed over her chest. "For the last time, we're not going to couples' therapy. Lady Shiba is a world-renowned relationship coach. She's been interviewed by Oprah and has been on some major shows. She's the real deal." Basil points at the entrance sign. "Her office is inside a botanical garden, for Christ's sake."

I don't know the difference between a relationship coach and a couple's therapist, but my opinion hasn't changed. About now, a polyamorous relationship's Google calendar sounds less stressful than the next forty-five minutes. "What are we going to talk about? Make up a bunch of stories and feelings about our relationship, which isn't real?

"All the details are inside the itinerary that you didn't bother reading." Basil slants a brow in my direction. "We're a happy couple on our honeymoon. How difficult will it be to act like two people who are madly, deeply in love?" A reassuring smile spreads across her lips.

I read the itinerary nights ago, but Basil doesn't need to know that. I'm rather enjoying these fits of selective outrage from my darling wife who seemingly tries to control everything and everyone.

"Just don't expect any deep conversations from me." Vulnerability might get me useful information for the case, which admittedly feels like a violation of privacy. Then again, perhaps intimate conversations are warranted from time to time. For professional reasons.

I exhale, letting the surrounding greenery release the tension around my shoulder blades. Sleeping on the stiff rattan sofa a foot shorter than me hasn't helped my already poor posture. Basil did offer to share the king-sized bed. Although there was more than enough space for two, I refused for obvious reasons.

I take in the cool morning air for a beat. Seeing two joggers reminds me that I haven't gone for a run since I left Seattle. The lack of my stress outlet is beginning to impact my psyche. I'll start again tomorrow before Basil wakes up.

"I'll go inside, but if that relationship coach wants to talk about our pasts, I'm out," I say when we turn the corner and see a small cobblestone building. After a glance at the nameplate against the rocky exterior, I squish my brows together. I wonder why she's called Lady Shiba.

We enter the room.

And get our answer.

I blink in disbelief. "Holy—"

"Jesus fuck," Basil blurts out, eyes as wide as mine, possibly betraying a similar horror. "Is that a life-sized Chia Pet?"

What am I looking at? At least it's a dog, not a hedgehog. Who knows what Basil's response to that would have been? She might've passed out. Too perplexed to answer the question, I inspect the massive green sculpture in the corner. As tall as the wall, it has large painted-black rocks for eyes and a coat made of succulents and moss. The details of its perky triangular ears and a curled tail are impressive, to say the least. I step further inside, and my attention shifts left, then right. We're alone, despite being watched by hundreds of beady little eyes. The walls are cluttered with posters, stuffed animals, and metal signs. Dog-shaped figurines are stacked like books on the bookshelves. Shiba Inus. I recognize the breed of dog. My cousin adopted one, years back. Runs a Shiba Inu social media group and everything. I'll keep that information to myself.

Now that I've captured the room in its entirety, the giant plant dog seems less out of place.

I search my brain for the right words. "This is a pretty—"

"Pretty unhealthy obsession?" Basil whispers.

"I was going to say 'eccentric space.'" Having had an artist for a mother, I'm versed in navigating floors littered with dried pallets, paintbrushes on plastic tarps, and pottery lining the walls.

A shuffling sound from behind the beaded curtain grabs my attention, a reminder of why I'm here. I pass the vintage orange couch facing the chair to stand next to Basil.

"Bienvenido! Welcome," a cheerful voice announces. "My apologies for being late. I had to take the pups outside. Please, take a seat." Enters the person I recall from reading the bio, an older woman with an olive complexion. Her wide grin shines as brightly as her highlighter-pink, shoulder-length hair. Her outfit matches the room's exuberance—turquoise glasses, a flowy gold skirt with ruffles, and a white blouse. Lady Shiba. Puerto Rico flag earrings dangle from her gauged ears.

Basil and I sit on the couch with Lady Shiba across from us.

"First things first. I start every session with a fun island fan favorite." She begins belting some song. "If you're sapphic and you know it, clap your hands." Lady Shiba claps twice. "If you're sapphic and you know it, clap your hands." Another two claps. There's an insistent nod in our direction, encouraging participation. No thanks. "If you're sapphic and you know it and you really love to show it. If you're sapphic and you know it…"

I slowly turn to Basil, a "What the fuck" look on my face. She responds with crinkled brows, then, using a finger, tilts my chin until I'm facing forward. She claps twice.

I shift in my seat as Lady Shiba reaches for maracas and starts from the beginning. Seconds later, she stops, a flare of pink in her cheeks at our parted-lip expressions. The music rehearsal ends, instruments returning to the table. "It grows on you."

A contemplative sound leaves Basil's lips, and she glides one leg over the other. "I'm sorry, we're not big on singing."

"What she said." I nod. I don't think I can last five more minutes of therapy or whatever this is.

"I understand." Lady Shiba offers a slow nod, whispering gibberish to herself before ending with, "Traits of a Shiba." She rises to her feet, giving off strong Rafiki-from-*The-Lion-King* vibes that make me wonder what plants are really on this island.

Lady Shiba turns her attention back toward us. "After reading your relationship energy, I know what you two need to succeed long-term. I'm going to teach you a short and simple exercise, then you may leave." She points to the floor cushions and instructs us to sit back to back.

Basil and I exchange looks. If doing this exercise means getting out of here without talking about our love life, I'll play along. I plop down first. Extending my long legs, I close my eyes, feeling Basil's presence as she sits.

"Backs touching, please," Lady Shiba insists. "This is a partner breathing exercise. One that's highly underrated, yet powerful. Seven minutes. No speaking, just breathing."

Basil shuffles behind me. I do the same until our backs are pressed together. I sense her tense energy and breathe through my own.

"Breathe. That's it?" I ask.

"That's it. Focus on being present for seven minutes. Through practice, this exercise will allow you to discover your unique synchronized rhythm. A two-person rowing team. That rich connection will guide you through any transformation." The beep of a timer sounds. "Begin."

I exhale through the flashing red lights in my brain, warning signs to end all of this honeymoon stuff with Basil. Sharing silence and breathing patterns seems more intimate than strolling down the shore holding hands at sunset would.

Giving in, I allow my shoulders and back muscles to sink and no longer resist Basil's essence. I could tell we are both focused on each other at the moment. The lull of her shallow breathing begins to settle my mind.

When time's up, we open our eyes, and I feel an emptiness in my core when she pulls away.

"Good. Keep practicing." Lady Shiba motions us to face each other. "And this exercise finishes with a seven-second kiss."

Silence.

My eyes go wide. "Oh, you mean right now? " I scramble to my feet. "PDA isn't really my thing. One of my quirks. Right, honey?"

"One of many," Basil responds, standing now. "We give you our word, we will complete this assignment later. With a high probability that it will exceed seven seconds. Because we are a happy couple on our honeymoon. Right, honey?" Her eyes meet mine.

I smile. "Right."

Lady Shiba laughs. "That's perfectly fine. Any further questions before we wrap up?"

I eye the door. "No return sessions?"

"A streak of stubborness in you, Caroline. Traits of a Shiba." Lady Shiba chuckles. "All I ask is that you perform this exercise any time your partner asks. Politely, of course. This only works with consent."

Ten minutes later, we're out the door.

I'm stuck wondering how a single thing from our session would benefit an actual couple? Then again, I'm far from a relationship "expert," only a firm believer in the wonders of naked cuddling.

Taking a stroll down the cement path toward the exit, I break the silence. "Are you sure that's the same person that was interviewed by Oprah?"

"Honestly, I don't know what to believe anymore." She chuckles. "Now that ridiculous song is stuck in my head. And don't get me started on that couples' breathing exercise."

"We're never doing that again." I shake my head. "What a waste of time."

"I concur."

I shake off the air between us, which now seems thicker since leaving Lady Shiba's office. Basil wasn't serious about the seven-second kiss...was she? My gaze drifts toward the ground as we continue walking. I catch myself reminiscing about her lips on mine and push the thought away. A run tomorrow is what I need to clear any residual sexual tension left from our hookup. I hope.

To break the silence, I sing the tune for no other reason than to get a rise out of Basil. "If you're sapphic and you know it—"

"Caroline!" She jokingly shoves my arm.

The corner of my mouth curls. "Think we can use, 'Doing very lesbian things' as an excuse to skip the rest of the scheduled events? Whatever that phrase means." She'll never live that one down.

Basil halts, hands on her hips. "You know *exactly* what I meant." Her eyes hold mine captive, just like the first time we met. "But you'll only see that sight again in your dreams."

"I better start sleeping, then." The words slip out of my mouth before I can catch them. "Sorry, I shouldn't have—"

"For the record, I'm not opposed to kissing you if the job description calls for it."

It's my turn to halt my footsteps. My brows shoot upward. "*That* certainly isn't on the itinerary." I barely hold back my laughter, peering over at her taken-aback response.

"You read it, didn't you?"

"The first night you handed it to me. All nineteen pages."

Her squinting, slack-jawed expression is priceless. She mocks Lady Shiba's voice. "Traits of a Shiba."

I tilt my head and smile. "What's wrong, honey? Not the kind of role-play you had in mind?"

Before she can respond, I lower my sunglasses over my eyes and step past, catching the slight curve in her lips as I do.

Several feet ahead now, I hum the song again—anything to get rid of the impure images canvassing my mind.

Stop thinking about her. No more flirting. No more touching. Focus on the job. Basil Jones is my target, and I already know what happens when I mix work with pleasure.

My heart gets destroyed.

CHAPTER 10

BASIL

"Have you let your freak flag fly yet?" Riley asks when I answer the phone.

On the deck, I take in the golden hour's warm amber hues. At least I can still enjoy this sight, even if the rest of my life is a mess. I can tell I'm on her car's Bluetooth and that she's stuffing her face with something. I bet it's an everything bagel. I miss our bagel, bags, and beer trips. I miss spending time with people who want me around, not people who are forced to be with me. Us talking reminds me of our morning commutes to work—she'd *talk*. I needed coffee to deal with her level of energy that early. We celebrated, gossiped, and laughed for an hour daily for months until her first lingerie line catapulted her business and I got promoted to VP at Elixir Wines.

"You're such a bad influence," I tease. I get it. Riley's attempting to distract me from ruminating, but Caroline and I had *one* night together, that's all. Granted, the sex was incredible, but what's the point in convoluting a situation that's already complicated? I sure as hell don't want another relationship.

"Seriously. I always say every woman's entitled to two things in life: toe-curling pleasure and one trashy TV show obsession."

"Does my life count as a trashy TV show?" I laugh, only partially joking.

"You're into her...aren't you?" There's a slow inflection in Riley's question. "Work and that one relationship consumed your twenties. No one is judging here if you need the distraction."

"The only thing I'm into is getting my life back on track. She's just..."

I think for a moment before continuing. Caroline's just... slowly consuming every thought I have? She's just gorgeous? Intelligent? Charming and oddly observant?

I return to the conversation. "She's just playing the part. Trust me, nothing will happen. The last thing on my mind is consummating my fake marriage."

"I mean, you two already started *something*. Maybe this is the universe handing you a divine sign...or at minimum, more orgasms. You're on the path to healing—nothing a little island fling can't help."

It feels like the entire island can hear our conversation. I twist around, hand covering my phone, and peer through the sliding doors. I'm relieved to discover no movement inside the villa.

I attempt to sort out my situation out loud. "First the wedding, then Caroline and I happened...then she happened *again*, Mock Honeymoon Edition. My client seems to love her. And to make matters worse, the Wicked Bitch of the West, Victoria Miller, is here." I exhale a breath. "Let's revisit the fact that I haven't swam or sunbathed or read a book once. It should be a crime, especially when I'm staying this close to the beach."

"Speaking of clients, my 8 a.m. appointment is standing in front of my door."

My thoughts wander as she talks with someone else. What would happen if I let myself enjoy this time with Caroline? Maybe Riley's right. I have a little over a week left on the island.

"Sorry, Basil." I tune back in when I hear her rustle her phone against her face. "My advice? Have fun. Just don't fall in love."

The call ends before I get my last words out: *I won't.*

CHAPTER 11

CAROLINE

I STILL CAN'T BELIEVE I'm working a surveillance case with my target within arm's reach, and now we're participating in the couples' Olympics. I'm trapped but can't deny my intrigue toward her.

Like yesterday, a slight breeze is combating the afternoon's blazing heat, making it perfect for outdoor activities. Depending on the person, I guess. Mamma would have refused to be out longer than an hour, calling today, "Sticky-shorts hot." Regardless, I'm the type of person who's rarely in the mood to go to an event but has fun once I'm there. I wonder if this tournament will be the same.

When we reach the beach, we stick our water bottles into the sand underneath a palm tree and join a group of couples stretching. I have no idea what I'm in for, but anything's better than Lady Shiba's shenanigans. I'm looking forward to being around people besides Basil. My thoughts have never been absorbed by another woman to this extent.

The area's packed with people congregating around several stations blocked off and covered by blue tarps. I catch wind of the couple standing next to us talking about piles of wood. Curiosity piqued, I grab the back of my neck. Are we building something? Then I wince in pain and groan. That couch will be the death of me. My body aches from sleeping on my side, and I'm hoping stretching will help. Basil's looking my way but doesn't say anything. I drop my arm before she makes a comment.

The smell of limes, beer, and grilled burgers fills my nose as we approach our station.

"There are a ton of people here. This must be a big deal," I say to Basil, noting we're the only couple not in matching uniforms.

"Now that the Joneses have arrived, this is more exciting than my love for stilettos, and that's saying something," Basil says.

I recall four high-dollar pairs neatly sitting near the closet door. "Let me guess, you don't like to lose?"

She shrugs. "I'm not the best at it. The bright side is if we lose, I'll get more time for sunbathing."

At that, I give her a slanted-brow look. I know she wouldn't dare let Lynn and Mae see her go down so easily.

"We won't be defeated. The only reason we lose is if we forfeit, so don't go entertaining any ideas." She sends me a playful wink.

"Thought so." I peek over at her outstretched body. As she reaches for the sky, her shirt rises enough for me to dance my sights along the gap of bare skin above her waistline. When she catches me, our eyes hold. I lean over to touch my toes and wince at the tightness in my hips.

"You okay?" Basil asks.

"Tiny-couch problems."

"You mean tall-woman problems." Her teasing grin finds me. "It doesn't go unnoticed."

A tingle travels up my spine as she slowly sizes me up. Using my towel, I wipe the beads of sweat forming on my forehead, then unstick the fabric from the back of my leg. It's officially sticky-shorts hot out here. I change the subject. "My hamstring gets tight after taking a few days off my exercise routine. Sleeping on a couch hasn't helped. I'm a stomach sleeper to boot."

"You mean I actually have to carry the team?"

My brows raise.

"Oh, don't give me that look. I offered the bed and you said no, remember?" A smile crosses her face before she takes a drink of water and returns to mocking me. "Poor honey dearest. Maybe try the floor? I'd ask if you want to share the bed again, but I'm getting used to all that space for myself, and if I remember correctly, you snore."

"You're a delight, you know that?"

She sandwiches her bottom lip between her teeth, her mouth curling upward. "A delight who wins."

I turn and take in the rushing waves rolling onto the shore. "At least the view's nice." Then I grumble, "Even if my wife isn't."

"Heard that," she fires back. "If charm were currency, you'd be bankrupt, honey."

I'm grinning at our back-and-forth, but I don't give her the satisfaction of seeing it.

Minutes later, we're ushered into position behind a line, cueing the announcer, an older black woman wearing an Afro and visor to approach the middle stage and tap the microphone. The show is about to begin.

In a Bruce Buffer style, the announcer belts the start of the Sapphic Olympics. Cheers and applause erupt all around us. So many women from all around the world are here. This is pride. This energy is special.

After a few lingering finger whistles, the crowd calms enough to clearly hear our instructions.

"I have incredible news for today's contestants!" The

announcer flashes a mischievous grin toward us. "The island's getting a boutique library that serves wine and sapphic books on tap for all to enjoy."

There's more clapping, and someone yanks the tarps away, exposing large cardboard boxes. "And *you're* going to help build the items that help make it possible."

Bookcases? I definitely didn't sign up for this.

"Serious question." Basil leans close after peering around, then whispers, "If we're all here, who's filling in at all the hardware stores? I've never seen this many tool-belt lesbians in one place."

I shrug and chuckle at her words. Then I watch confusion stir amongst the teams as heads turn, possibly just as thrown off as we are.

There's maniacal laughter from the announcer. "Only the top teams advance to the next round. Your assignment is to build a bookcase. Simple enough, right? Now, let's get this party started."

I huff. "More like divorce party. I know couples who barely make it out of IKEA alive."

"This is hardly a challenge." Basil straightens her back. "All we have to do is build one bookcase."

"Right." Timed, competing against several couples with hundreds of people watching…

The bell dings, interrupting my train of thought. Shouts roar against the summer breeze, commanding my limbs into motion. Sounds of ripping cardboard fill the air as boxes come undone. Outside the long plastic sheet holding the various screws and tiny parts. There's not many pieces. Simple enough.

That's where "simple" ends.

I watch Basil stick her nose into the instruction manual first and begin organizing the parts into groups. *Miserably* slowly. I don't know why I care about winning. Then again,

I'm not great at losing either—not games, and not people. After plopping my butt onto the sand, I position the empty box on its side and stare at the picture, then pick up the screwdriver and start attaching two pieces together.

"That doesn't go together," I hear Basil yell.

It's not rocket science. "Yes, it does."

I tighten another screw into the pre-drilled hole. She comes over and, with two fingers, grabs the thin piece of wood back from my hand and adds it to a pile. "Step one: the As go adjacent to the Es. But we need to make sure we have all the parts first. Otherwise this is futile."

"The image is straightforward. Most times, companies give you extra pieces."

She continues taking inventory mumbling something. I can only decipher the words, "not idiot proof." Meanwhile, I pull another A from the pile and grab the Allen wrench. "We don't have time for the instructions. I don't need them. I'll look at the picture."

"Ever heard the saying 'measure twice, cut once'?" Her tone doesn't curb my increasing annoyance. She points at the paper, the line that says to not fully tighten the screws until the end. "By taking shortcuts, you're risking failure. Instructions are made for a reason. The perfect end solution."

"Perfection doesn't necessarily equal competency," I fire back without making eye contact. "Sometimes, you need to do whatever it takes to get the job done."

She dismisses my words and continues skimming the paperwork. Then she walks over, brows scrunched in confusion. "Those two don't go together until step five. Again, the instructions say to not fully tighten the screws until step—"

I let out an audible sigh. "We're wasting time."

If only Basil's itinerary contained common sense on furniture assembly.

"We didn't hire people to put together anything for us." I

study the picture on the box once more. "My dad was in the military. We moved around a lot and I got good at doing this."

"Oh and you think I haven't built anything before? We both know I'm not exactly a pillow princess."

"That's not what I meant." I know from her case file, the property values alone, that her family has money. Maybe I shouldn't judge her from the family life she didn't choose to be born into, but I push the thoughts away. We're running out of time and aren't halfway done.

Finally, I retract my hand from reaching for a tool and meet Basil's gaze. "Not all of us had the luxury of never getting our hands dirty. I wouldn't be surprised if you hadn't built a single piece of furniture a day in your life."

"Wow. You're making quite the assumption about me." She squints a glare. "I've built plenty, thank you. In fact, I'm helping build a business empire. I've also organized events worth more than one *thousand* bookcases."

"Right."

"How many businesses have you built?" Her lips compress.

"I—"

A whistle sounds, then another. Cheers erupt as more couples finish, filling slots to advance. I look up and see a couple dramatically arguing and flaring their arms, screaming at each other, which makes me feel better. Some woman named Bear stomps away. The only reason I know her name is because the other woman with black hair just screamed it. The crowd is loving the hot-mess drama. The same woman marches after this Bear person, only to be met with a middle finger. Clearly a forfeit. At least we aren't *that* embarrassing. Yet time's clicking by, and Basil and I are still bickering like an old couple. For what? She needs me, not the other way around.

"Fine." I drop the bag of parts and brush the sand from my hands. "Put it together yourself, but don't be a sore loser because you took too long."

She scoffs. "Don't try reverse psychology on me. *You* put it together, and when it falls to shambles or you can't blow the whistle, I'll be here to tell you, 'I told you so.'"

I shake my head and mutter a choice word under my breath.

Basil stands over me, arms crossed over her chest. "I bet you can't finish on time."

Now, *that* is hilarious.

She mocks a smile in return. "I'll give you half the bed if you do. But you won't."

I yank my head back and raise both eyebrows. Did she just challenge me? Psh. Tell me what I can't do and I'll prove the world wrong. "You're on, honeybuns."

Another whistle blows behind us. Two women walk off hand in hand, and the crowd goes wild at their celebratory kiss.

"Watch me and weep," I tell Basil.

She takes two steps back and tilts her head, a sly grin slowly forming across her face. Then it hits me.

Wait a minute.

What did I just agree to? Did she just pull some re-reverse psychology on me or something? Damn it. She's good.

Suddenly, it feels like the entire island is watching me. I refuse to sit here and look like a bigger idiot than I already feel. I glance at the timer sitting on the table, mustering up any remaining pride, and reach for the screwdriver.

Next thing I know, there are less than three minutes left. It's a miracle I'm still in the running to advance to the next round.

My faux wife flashes a thumbs-up at me, then returns to

the task at hand. Standing there. Watching the others, arms folded, feet not moving an inch.

The announcer states the obvious. This is coming down to the wire.

"You might want to hurry," Basil says and points to the couple in front of us. "They're almost finished."

I bolt to my feet. "I'm done, I'm done. I just need the—" I rush toward the cardboard box, flip it upside down and dig through styrofoam, sheets of plastic flying everywhere. "Where the hell is it?"

"Lose something?" She walks closer. "Do you want my help?"

"No. I got it." I drop to my knees and frantically push the sand around.

"You sure?" she adds when we lock eyes briefly, fighting the grin teasing the corner of her mouth. "What are you looking for?"

I grunt in frustration. "The stupid whistle. I can't find—"

A loud shrill echoes through the air, followed by an explosion of cheers.

I step into the room and place my bag on the chair. I'm exhausted and will probably be discovering sand in places it shouldn't be for days after my shower. I look down at my shorts and T-shirt. It's not like I'm sleeping naked or anything. I sit on the side of the bed closest to the door.

The shower cuts off, and ten minutes later, Basil steps into the bedroom. My chest tightens, and my eyes redirect to every spot inside the room except her body. My gaze points to the floor. Does she seriously expect me to sleep with her looking like *that*?

"What are you doing?" I ask.

"Going to bed."

"Wearing that?" Dealing with the woman's sass is one thing, but being in the same room while black and pink lace cover her breasts is a different type of torture.

A whiff of rose-oil body wash fills my nose as she passes me en route to her side of the bed, facing the sliding doors. I silently watch her shove pillow after pillow onto the bed, forming a wall down the middle. I can't redact my victory now, especially that she's tossed me the whistle *and* is still holding up her end of the bet. Kindness looks good on her.

Her brow crinkles when our eyes hold, a tiny smirk on her lips. "What? Haven't seen a woman in sleepwear before?"

I bite back my smartass response and choose different words. "So, we're just going to pretend you aren't sleeping in lingerie. With a total stranger?"

"We're hardly strangers. You've had your tongue in my—"

"I mean, we don't know much about each other." Actually, she knows nothing about me.

She sees how serious I am and drops her arms. "Sorry to break it to you, but this is what I packed. I was planning for a honeymoon, remember?"

I can tell when she pulls her eyes away and frowns at the wall that she's thinking about something. Or someone.

"Look." Basil clears her throat. "The floor's right there if you change your mind." Two pillows land at my feet, and she crawls into the bed. "Or…just keep your hands and lips away. And you'll be fine." The lamp clicks off.

Surrounded by darkness, I pause to think. Maybe the floor is a better option. The rug is softer than one would expect. My back aches at the thought of sleeping on another hard surface. I can do a pillow wall, can't I? Kaydence once told me, "You're as great of an emotional wall builder as you are a private investigator." Surviving a half dozen pillows is nothing. Sleeping in the same bed as my target, who I find a little attractive...okay, more than a little...isn't ideal, but everything will be fine. No rules have been broken. *You can handle a pillow wall, Caroline.* The words circle my mind again and again.

After letting out an exhale in defeat, I yank the pillows from the floor, add the fluffy rectangles back to the pillow wall, then carefully slide underneath the sheets.

Satisfied, I sigh, melting further into the mattress, and close my eyes.

"Good job today."

"Thank you for pointing out the whistle was taped to the instructions." And by nearly giving me a heart attack in the process. She proved her point, I suppose.

"Believe me, I know what it's like to get screwed over by someone you were supposed to build something with." Basil rustles into position and yawns. "With your resilience, you might be cut out to be a Jones after all."

"Are you kindly pointing out my stubbornness?"

"Same difference."

Silence.

"You adapt while being persistent. That's resilience, and I appreciate you for it."

I can't help my smile. An herb joke for good measure. "Thanks for the encourage-mint." I mimic her laughter. "Good night, Basil."

She chuckles, voice thick with sleep. "Night."

CHAPTER 12

BASIL

I TOSS and turn from my stomach to my side, then from my side back to my stomach. The pillow-between-the-legs trick hasn't worked, and neither have the sleep mask and ear plugs from the airline. Just when I feel myself drifting, sleep about to take hold, the front door clicks shut, meaning it has to be approximately six-thirty in the morning. Caroline is gone, exercising for an hour or so. At least someone has been getting decent rest.

"Fuck it," I grumble and snap my eyes open, welcoming the all-too-familiar burnt-orange hues of the sunrise peeking through the sheer curtains. I rise from the bed, put on the T-shirt Caroline handed me last night, grab my romance novel, and step toward the deck. Watching the sunrise at least one time made its way on my to-do list, and I'll check that box, even if that means with my new book girlfriend and not Olivia.

The morning air's humidity is mild. Warm and comfortable, but I can sense that won't last for long. With a towel down, I lower onto the lounge chair, and within minutes of reading, a heat wave courses through my body. The same heat has often traveled between my thighs when I'm indulging in the world I crave, though I've suppressed my desire for exploration for Olivia's sake. When it happened, our sex was pleasurable, predictable, safe, much like the rest of my life until late—but oftentimes, I have found myself craving more.

Back on the plane, I recall clamping my book shut, unable to continue, as if the entire metal tube holding over two hundred people could read each salacious word that I was reading. Not only do the many delicious ways my book girlfriend serves sexual torment get me hot all over, we share similar struggles—misunderstood, newly single, and desperately avoiding the inevitable walk across the plank bridge from Broken Heart Boulevard.

The sleepy fog that meddles with my mind melts, deepening the sensual fantasy. A soft, midnight-colored rope binds the other woman's arms and legs to the bed posts. I welcome each enticing touch as if they are painting my own skin, my limbs at my book girlfriend's mercy. Fingers hover dangerously close, down my forearms, as whispered words reach my ears. A soft, yet commanding voice taunts me. "I can't wait to taste you…but you're going to have to wait."

The tip of a woman's tongue brushes along the most delicate spots of my neck, down the valley of my breasts before gently tugging on my right nipple. There is only so much teasing a person can stand before begging for release—something I haven't experienced in far too long.

No longer able to ignore the increasing pulsing sensation between my legs, I cautiously look around to verify I am alone on a private deck. I slip my free hand underneath the oversized T-shirt, then between the layer of black lace panties and my hot skin. I consider the safety of the shower, then remember the island has everything except a damn removable shower head. Besides that, a different type of sexual confidence stirs within me, along with a desire to create new memories. Ones that thoughts of Olivia won't ruin.

Still somewhat hesitant, my fingers linger along my panty line, but as soon as my fictional girlfriend drifts south, so do my fingers. There is not enough alone time to bring myself to the edge, to yank back, then repeat like a powerful release requires. I want to come fast, feel invigorated and relieve some tension.

The tongue returns, only teasing my outer lips for a moment, before delving through my wetness and changing rhythm. In response, I stroke V-shaped fingers down, then up, hugging my swollen clit. A tiny moan exits my slightly gaped mouth from the satisfying touch.

My nipples harden, poking firmly against the fabric of my shirt. The imaginary arm reaches up, and not-so-gentle fingers knead one of my bare breasts as flicks of the tongue increase, lapping with urgency. I match with strokes fueled with purpose. Sounds of breaking waves take a back seat to my breathing, which grows tattered as I please myself. Remaining hyperfocused on my route to orgasm, I let go, surrendering to the mouth devouring me.

The book drops to the side. I clamp my eyes shut, dip my head back, and, using two fingers, rub in quick, tight circles. Breathy moans escape while fire blazes inside me from the soft lips sucking me, the deliberate pinching on my rock-solid nipple making my hips buck, legs contracting and testing the restraints. I gasp, taking in scents of salt from the ocean as air enters my nose, ripples of my orgasm trans-forming into crushing waves.

Lost in the fantasy, I meet the carnivorous dark eyes of the woman bringing me to bliss. When I do, Caroline's face appears. I love this view as her tongue fucks me, penetrating gaze intense on mine. I miss her touch, how in tune she was with my body. Denying them or a release is no longer an option, and sleeping next to one another isn't enough. I'm craving for her to touch me and would gladly return the favor. In the safety of my mind, the memories of Caroline King's glorious tongue bring me closer to the edge, and with one final stroke, a deep moan escapes my throat, and I cry out.

CHAPTER 13

CAROLINE

Now *this is* what I'm talking about. My body's buzzing from the sight of two women standing on round platforms in the center of a massive red mat on the beach. Tiki torches flicker against the sunset, outlining the arena. I peer around and nod in approval. Here's a sport I enjoy sweating over. The next round of the Sapphic Olympics is looking up after all.

While Basil sits next to me, eyes glued to the on-going match, intently watching every strike, block and weave, mine are on her. The third time I catch myself staring and return to people watching.

"What is this?" she asks. "Looks like we went from a home-improvement show to some type of survival game. Whatever we're doing, I hope we start before it gets dark."

"Gladiator Strike. We used to play every once in a while during boot camp." My lips curl into a grin as I recollect memories of my victorious bouts against Kaydence. With us both being masculine-presenting Black women, people would often confuse us during training. I created a distinction. A type of legacy during my military days with Gladiator Strike. When I update Kaydence on case details later, I'll remind her, since bragging rights don't have expiration dates. Basil studies the equipment, seemingly attempting to picture the mechanics, so I explain.

"You stand on that stool-looking thing, holding the Q-tip-looking poles with heavy pads at the ends, called pugil sticks, and joust until someone falls."

"Joust? Like *American Gladiator?*" She seems to understand when I nod, then follows me toward our corner, where two red pugil sticks and helmets sit. "That's a bit barbaric."

"And extremely fun." While stretching, I think about Basil's short frame compared to our competition, who look like models cut out from a fitness magazine. I'm prepared for this game. Basil, who's still fumbling and sliding into equipment behind me, might be another story. "It can get intense, even with the head protection, especially with the rapid shots I deliver. If you want, I can show you a thing or two—"

Whack. Whack. Whack.

I twist around, eyes wide, and watch Basil glare at the human dummy doll. Her knees are bent, feet squared in ready position. "Looks like you've done this before," I yell.

"Nope." There's a powerful strike to the sand-filled bag, then she winds up and hammers down like she's splitting a log in half with an axe. *Whack.*

Or perhaps she has pent-up anger. Understandably so.

After a few more blows to the torso, she drops the stick and uses the bottom of her tank top to wipe the sweat on her forehead. Of course I noticed. Breathing heavily, she walks over and nods toward our opponents. "I'm ready. You take the one on the right. She looks more your speed."

I analyze the shorter woman warming up. I have at least half a foot on her. "Are you sure about that?"

"You don't believe I can take the one on the left?"

"She's about my height and looks pretty intense. I just feel like you'd be better matched up with the other one."

She places her hands on her hips. "You want another bet, don't you?"

Based on the mischief in her eyes, I can only imagine what we'd bet on next. "I never said that."

She passes me the pugil stick and watches me do a few practice swings. I pause until the right words come to me. "No one on this island is as strong as Robo Arms 3000 over there."

"Sounds like someone's worried about my wellbeing."

I meet her sarcasm with a playful glare, then wield my own. "We can make this more interesting if you'd like."

"I bet we don't go to three matches." No third match means she's assuming I'll beat my opponent and that she'll beat hers. What is she planning this time? A determined smile creeps across her face. "If we both win, you come to the beach with me."

I make a buzzer noise. "No thanks. I'm not interested in being your personal lifeguard and drink server."

"How about a beach date after the couples' massage? My way to apologize for ditching you back in Seattle. And I'd like to spend more time with you."

A deep-tissue massage sounds amazing for my body right about now. I'm looking forward to that tomorrow. "You might have to sweeten this deal for me."

Her eyes drift to my lips, then back up. "What do you want?"

You. The word hangs in the air between us as my mind wanders to places I'd normally go for a salacious response, but I hold my tongue. I face the ocean and think logically. It's not like I technically have a choice. Where she goes, I go. At least that's what I'll keep telling myself.

"Actually, I just realized—" I turn back around, exaggerating my wide-mouthed expression. "You're asking me on a date *and* apologizing? Are you feeling okay?"

"You do realize you still need to actually win first."

"Have you no faith?" I match her coy grin with a side eye.

I put on the headgear and tighten the chin strap. Picking up a red pugil stick, I march toward the platform, conveniently not stopping the firm padding from swatting Basil's left butt cheek as I pass. When I look back at her open-jawed grin, I smile mischievously and shrug. "Oops."

Before she rebuts, the same announcer from the first game starts her spiel. This is the largest, fiercest crowd we've encountered yet. I'm not sure why, but I fist pump the air, excitement coursing through me when the game I had in mind is confirmed. Gladiator Strike. Perhaps the nature of competition brings out my fighting spirit. I'm up first, then Basil, and if it comes down to a tie-breaker, each team will select their third-round fighter.

I place my sunglasses in my bag and rise to my feet. "I overheard that the Bellini Babes team are the reigning Sapphic Olympics champions for the third year in a row. They had a quick win this morning. Broke their own record."

"Seems like the team to beat, then. We'll have to keep winning to see them." Basil grumbles more words I can't hear. "Let's recap," she says. "You take the short-haired one, I'll take the redhead. Look alive out there."

I nod and climb onto the platform. Before realizing the bell rang, I get struck on the side of the head. I shake it off and refocus.

Turns out Basil was right. My opponent is quick, dipping and blocking against my signature rapid jabs. The round is a long and rigorous battle, one that makes beating Kaydence seem like cake, and that was no easy feat. Stamina from jogging has paid off, though, and my opponent's blitz offense fizzles out. I find an opening, and I muster enough strength for a final strike to the shoulder. My opponent loses her balance and plummets toward the mat.

The whistle blows.

I'm struggling to breathe, plenty glad the round is over. While victoriously holding the stick above my head, I take in the cheers erupting in my favor.

The pain of competing against an athlete who appears fifteen years younger sets in shortly after. Before my wobbly legs give out, staff hands assist me moving my heavy limbs off the platform and into a chair. Basil removes the headgear, and a staff member hands over a water bottle, then offers a pat on the back. Hair sticks to my forehead. Clothes drenched in sweat, I blink continuously until a dimpled grin comes into clear focus. It is a glorious sight.

"You had me a little worried for a second." Basil crouches down inches away from my face, scanning me from eye to eye like a doctor. "You really don't quit, do you?"

I take a drink, long enough for my pounding heartbeat to slow. "I've never quit anything in my life, and I don't intend to start now."

Following her line of vision, I twist my torso to see Lynn and Mae frantically waving. We crack up laughing at Lynn's Viking-style helmet with beer cans resting inside each horn and a thin plastic tube dangling near her mouth.

Basil's up next.

Cheers sound, yanking my attention toward the arena. The two women stand still for only a second before the whistle blows. Blue lands the first strike, hitting Basil's side. A loud, dull thud echoes. It hurt. Her grimace confirms. Another whack to the shoulder. Basil's foot slips off the edge. The crowd gasps. Helpless, I wince, wishing I could do something.

Somehow, Basil fixes her footing in time and twists to the side, dodging a strike toward the shin. Then it's like a switch flips inside her mind. She delivers strike after strike. The crowd's chanting seems to fuel her as she swings, blitzing blows to the woman's torso, then a powerful swing at the side of her head. The woman topples off the platform.

I check the time. All that in less than fifteen seconds? The announcer shouts, and the crowd goes wild.

She tied the Bellini Babes' record.

"Okay, I see you out there, Gladiator Jones." Once Basil is seated in front of me, I hold a hand up, and she meets my high five with an toothy grin, displaying that adorable dimple. "Now that was impressive. We should change our team name to Jousting Joneses."

Basil laughs. "I think I found my calling." She takes a deep breath. "God, I needed that. I feel incredible."

"Have fun?" I ask, already knowing the answer.

"That was better than sex." She giggles and wrangles her flyaways, pulling the hair tie from between her teeth, and wraps her hair into a messy bun. "Where has Gladiator Strike been all my life? Great stress relief."

I crack a smile. It's been a while since I've felt high on the sheer joy of competition. Certainly Basil is experiencing it too. For the first time, our team doesn't feel so fake, even if our marriage status says otherwise.

I can't help my grin widening as I watch her soak up the praise. I'd never seen Basil so...happy. Thinking for a moment, I can't remember the last time I had this much fun with another woman. Not even with Grace.

"Come on, Gladiator Jones." I redirect Basil's attention left. "You won't want to miss the fans heading our way."

"Good job out there!" Lynn approaches first, slipping her arms around both our torsos and pulling us into a tight hug. "Remind me not to get on Basil's bad side." When she lets go, Mae catches up to the group.

"Not bad for your first Olympic go-around." Lynn side-hugs Basil again. "Not going to lie, I thought you were chopped liver, but Mae had zero doubts." Lynn, being Lynn, uses her fist as a microphone. "Mrs. Jones, please share the secret sauce of today's victory."

"Secret sauce?" Not missing a beat, Basil repeats into the pretend microphone like a professional athlete. "Easy. I imagined I was hitting the head of one of the Bellini Babes." Her smile turns coy. "Respectfully."

"Oooh," Lynn roars. "The semifinals are going to be *interesting*."

The conversation shifts to wine industry news until it's time to say our goodbyes. Lynn extends an invitation to get drinks with some of the Tier One members, but Mae gives us an out, which Basil and I graciously take. I can already sense the onset of soreness in muscles I forgot existed.

Light from the remaining sun hovering above the horizon casts shadows against women scattered on the beach. The island comes alive in the evening. Music plays in the distance, and clanking bottles and laughter pierce the air.

Lynn and Mae stay for a moment longer, seeming relaxed and content with the evening. Basil and I share a smile, glancing at Lynn rocking her wife in her arms.

"Let's snap a couple of pictures for the emerging champs before we go." Lynn pecks Mae's neck before pulling away. "Memories and all that."

"Of course," Mae says. "I'll use one of your phones, if you prefer, or I can use mine."

Basil's turns to me. "It's okay, no need—"

Lynn interjects. "No big deal. She can text them to you."

A wave of panic sets in. The last thing I need are pictures of Basil and me, cozy, out in the universe. My *target*. Knowing Lynn, next week they'll be added to Goddess Lagoon's webpage.

"Here," I speak up, and I dig through my bag and hand my phone over.

Mae proceeds to take a number of photos. Lynn insists on a silly one.

"All right, last one," Mae announces. "Basil. Caroline. How about a kissing photo for the album?"

"Ooh, a victory kiss," Lynn adds. "Brilliant. You're in great hands. Mae is an excellent photographer. "

My wide-eyed expression meets Basil's. The PDA excuse comes to mind. "I don't do—"

My words cut off at Basil's stern headshake. She faces the Blakemans. "Thank you so much for the kind offer—"

"We understand how hard it can be to capture the mushy moments, especially outside of the island. People come to Sapphire Isle from all over the world because it's a safe space. If that's of concern." When we don't object, Mae motions us to move closer. "Quickly now. Not much light left."

Swift to act, I face Basil and bring one of her hands inches from my lips. We lock eyes, and I plant a gentle kiss across her knuckles. An engagement-photo pose I saw on an internet ad. Not one I thought I'd ever perform. After what feels like forever, I retract my mouth and slowly let go of her hand. Basil's expression is unreadable.

Lynn exaggerates a heartfelt, "Aww." She and Mae share a moment.

"That was adorable, but don't stop acting like newlyweds just because we're around," Lynn says. "Enjoy yourselves. Give her a win-worthy smooch, Caroline."

My body tenses. It's not that I don't want to or wouldn't if she were my wife. I shouldn't because she's my target. "I'm all sweaty and—"

"Go ahead. Only if you want." Basil's voice is soft, a faint blush in her cheeks.

"Okay, yeah." Nervous, I play with my fingers, almost despising Lynn for acting like a nosy family member during the holidays. Basil offers a reassuring smile and, using two fingers, pulls my shirt and me closer.

Mae holds up the phone again. A proud parent taking prom photos.

Butterflies are swarming through my belly as I step forward. It's as if I'm a teenager having my first kiss again. But this isn't Basil and my first by a long shot. There was *nothing* shy between us before. This feels bigger than the case. Maybe I'm afraid of what will happen after we kiss again. Grace made promises only to go back on them. Am I avoiding the pain of wanting someone I can't have?

Giving into the magnetism between us forces me to acknowledge the flame lingering in my chest for Basil, regardless of if I want it there or not. Feelings just are. I remind myself we're doing this for show. At first, I wonder why she hasn't objected, then it hits me. This moment has been inevitable since the first day I stepped inside the villa.

"Okay," I whisper again and lick my lips, then let myself get lost in her azure-irises. I tip her chin up and pause briefly, searching her eyes for self-restraint, but neither of us can find it. Our lips brush, and the softness and her familiar taste overwhelm me. I'm zapped back to the last time we kissed—how badly I wanted her then and how royally screwed I am now.

Just as I'm pulling away, her lips press firmly against mine, taking me by surprise. We part, our eyes hold, and my pulse jolts against my skin.

Shit. I've crossed a professional line here—and knowing it does nothing to stop my increasing desire to kiss her again.

CHAPTER 14

BASIL

IT'S THE NEXT DAY, and kissing Caroline hasn't left my mind. After finishing breakfast at the resort's restaurant, Caroline and I stop and study the directory to locate the spa. Given today's wide-open schedule, outside of our couples' massage, we have time to rejuvenate from the packed itinerary we've endured. No Olympics today, unless sunbathing counts as a sport. While Caroline was showering last night, I called the front desk to arrange a romantic lunch-date package. Sunny took my order, and we had a surprisingly nice conversation. I can't deny the fact that she provided excellent suggestions. I can respect a person who has great taste in decor and wine choices. Maybe she's not too bad.

Coming back to the present, I chuckle, struggling to keep up as Caroline leads the way, her long legs pacing toward our destination. This is the most excitement I've witnessed from her. While I'm usually the one reminding her of the time, this morning, she was waiting for me by the door. A smile as bright as her sunflower-colored tank top was plastered across her lips. Understandably so. I've been looking forward to this massage since I booked it over a year ago.

I overhear voices from the hallway we're traveling down. There's giggling like that from a couple of giddy teenagers. Seconds later, two women dressed in matching white linen robes turn the corner. I roll my eyes. Victoria Miller again. Can't I have one day of peace and not be constantly reminded of the past?

"If it's not Seattle's finest." Victoria's sarcasm rings loud and clear.

"Vicky," I state matter-of-factly. "Funny, we keep running into each other. I'm beginning to wonder if it's intentional."

"I would say we're scouting you, but I don't want to give off the impression that you have a chance at beating us."

"You're in the tournament?" Caroline asks with a wide smile, as if she's attempting to break the tension. "Didn't know that. Which team?"

Victoria bursts with that hideous laughter that makes my skin itch. "The one and only Bellini Babes." Lauren meets her fist bump. "Three-time champions. And as of 9 a.m. yesterday, the official PR agency for the Blakemans. You know them, correct?"

What? I squint a glare. "You won't win a fourth. I guarantee you that." Her *head* has inflated times three since we've last seen each other. She's acting as if I didn't just tie her Gladiator Strike record on my first try. The thought of being remotely connected with her in any way irritates me. I recall Hazel telling me she forgave Victoria years ago, following it up with some lofty speech about closure, but I believe some things shouldn't be forgiven.

She huffs. "I couldn't hear you over the sound of your mediocrity." She seems amused with herself. "It's cute you think you're playing in the same league."

"I'd love to hear more about your accomplishments, but I don't have a magnifying glass handy."

Victoria crosses her arms over her chest. "Try not to be a

pesto-mistic bitch when you lose. Better yet, drop out of the tournament. It's your only way to avoid becoming a bigger embarrassment than you already are."

My jaw clenches. I hand Caroline my to-go coffee and search for as careful of words as I can when I'm eye-to-eye with a malicious woman wearing a sundress.

"Look here, Bellini Bimbo," I growl, despising that I've let her get underneath my skin. "Keep talking. Eventually, you might say something intelligent."

"*Okay*, you two. Let's be adults," Caroline intervenes, gently tugging at my arm. Meanwhile, Lauren looks baffled beyond belief. "Our massage starts any minute now. Come on, Basil."

"Enjoy your massage. Perhaps when it's over, you'll have acquired a touch of civility." Victoria flashes an exaggerated fake smile. Walking past, she pauses her footsteps and lowers her voice. "I've been watching you, Jones. I'd be careful unless you want your little secret to reach the Blakemans. Quit the tournament or else."

Lauren opens her mouth to speak, but hesitates, a pained look on her face. "I'm sorry...for her."

They're gone.

The air escapes my lungs, and my nails dig into my palms, forming tight fists. Blackmailing me over a *trophy*? Would she stoop so low as to use my heartbreak against me to make herself look good? I cannot believe the Blakemans hired that vile woman's PR company. She clearly has them fooled. I mean, I'm no saint, lying about my marriage, but still, I'd never—

"Hey." Caroline's soft hand touching mine halts my train of thought. Her voice is a low hum. "Are you okay?"

When I meet her calming brown eyes, I feel a tear well up and turn my body before it falls. I wipe my cheek. "I'm fine. God, I cannot stand her."

"Can't say I'm a fan myself. What happened between you two? You seem to hate each other."

My glare points down the hallway. "It's old news. Nothing she didn't deserve."

Caroline slowly nods. Thankfully, she gets the hint to drop the topic and exhales a breath. "We can reschedule the massage for another day if you don't feel up for one."

Victoria's words invade my mind. Should I give up and drop out of the tournament? None of this would be happening if I hadn't lied in the first place—to myself, to the Blakemans, to Caroline. I had always seen myself as ruthlessly ambitious, not caring about what others thought of me, but maybe it's the opposite? Do I care too much? I've wanted to be the perfect businesswoman, wife, and daughter, and right now, I feel like I'm failing at all three.

"Today's fine," I say eventually. "A relaxing massage is what I need to rid myself of the stench named Victoria Miller."

After checking in, we're escorted inside a dim, minimally decorated room. Soothing rainfall music whispers alongside the tranquil ambience. I face the center and freeze. Caroline matches my open-jawed expression at the sight of only one massage table. I glance toward the door and check the sign. That's my last name. How'd I miss such a critical word on my itinerary? There's a substantial difference between a couples' massage and a couples' massage *class*.

Twenty minutes later, I'm hovering above Caroline's naked body, which is covered by a blanket. My hands, slick with oil, gliding across her warm, toned thighs isn't quite how I pictured my day going, but I'm not complaining. I recall how long she teased me with her tongue on our first night together. How wild she drove me in a matter of seconds, and here's my chance to repay the favor. Remembering we're not alone, I fight my mind to stay present, avoiding letting the instructions fall into the background with each stroke, knead, and tap on her muscles. Based on the soft moans slipping from her mouth, she seems quite pleased with my efforts. The way she's expressing that pleasure is doing things to my neurons. Admittedly, I think I'm enjoying this more than she is.

After she flips onto her back and closes her eyes, I retrieve more oil, then smile at the sign on the wall. *Couples who massage together, stay together.* Noted.

I position myself behind her head and study the contours of her face. It's the first time I've slowed down and taken in her beauty since the morning in Seattle. Her body is breathtaking, and her skin is vibrant and rich as a vineyard in full harvest. As if sensing me staring, her eyelids lazily flip open, meeting mine. I want to kiss her, but it seems inappropriate. As my thumbs knead the full length of the sides of her neck, she murmurs how good it feels, sending a heat wave throughout my body. I *really* like pleasing her.

When the class is almost over, the massage therapist advises us that the remaining time is ours. She quietly exits the room, leaving us alone.

As I continue rubbing Caroline's top half, my mind goes back to her "accidentally" swatting my butt with the pugil stick yesterday. She's fun to be around, even when we disagree.

We remain quiet while I return to her shoulders, then sensually slide my hands closer, teasing the line of the linen across her chest. Her skin is heating up against my fingertips as desire courses through my veins.

A smile tugs at the corners of her lips. "Don't start anything you can't finish. You don't have to try to turn me on. A little late for that."

That makes two of us. "I remember plenty of finishing

happening between us." I dip down and find her ear. "Did you think I would let yesterday's little stunt slide?"

Her soft chuckle sounds the same as the one during our late-night talks before we fall asleep. "Which one?"

Taking both hands, I slip underneath the blanket and knead her breasts, rolling her hardening nipples against my palm. When she lets out a breathy moan, I pull away and lower my voice. "Oops."

She bites her bottom lip and huffs a laugh. "Watch your six. I know where you sleep."

Yes, and that pillow wall feels like the side of a castle that I want to bulldoze.

"Did you think I was referring to our kiss yesterday?" I ask curiously. "Although I wouldn't consider it a proper kiss." Still standing behind her head, I form a loose C with my hands and pull inward on the tops of her shoulder muscles, adding just the right amount of firm pressure with my thumbs.

She lets out a satisfied sigh. "That feels amazing." Her hooded eyes find mine, a teasing grin on her face. "Are you going to remind me what's considered proper, then?"

I pause my hands and hold her gaze. "Since you asked…" Slowly, I lower and brush our lips together. I feel her smile against mine, and we lock lips again. This time, I deepen the kiss. Remembering how good she feels, I melt into her touch. When she runs her tongue along my top lip, the throbbing between my thighs quickens as I welcome her. Our tongues dance at a steady rhythm until we part for air.

"I think Spider-Man would be jealous," she whispers.

I take in the alluring dark eyes that make my thoughts melt away once more, then I add space between us, recalling that we need to leave this room in a few minutes and that I only have one pair of panties on hand. "If only my hands literally shot webs, we'd be an unstoppable team."

Using her long arms, she pulls me in for another kiss. "Or you could launch one over Victoria's mouth."

That's a wonderful mental image. Nothing could stop my grin at this moment. Maybe Riley was right when she said to have fun. I plant a kiss on her hand. "I love it when you talk dirty to me."

That makes her laugh. "If you think *that* was dirty talk, you're in big trouble."

Smiling, my mind flashes back when I was lying on the deck reading my book, getting swept away in a fantasy involving Caroline's skillful tongue. "I can only hope."

CHAPTER 15

CAROLINE

"How's the vacation?" Kaydence asks during our video chat. I switch my phone camera to point at the beach and slowly move my hand side to side, showing the clear blue water from the deck.

"Enjoying another perfect afternoon." A grin forms across my lips watching her and Rosie's faces light up in awe. She eases Rosie down from her lap to go play. As a part of my godmother duties, once a week I video chat with the little one. Actually, Rosie sneaks into Kaydence's bag and starts pressing buttons on her phone. Regardless, I'm always delighted to see her adorable, tiny face. Kaydence and I are due for an update anyhow. With most of our cases, check-ins are on an as-needed basis; however, this client's high-dollar sign and perks come with high demands, including daily, comprehensive reports. Thankfully, Kaydence handles those.

"So, married life is for you after all?"

"I wouldn't go that far." I scoff, not wanting to look like I'm enjoying myself more than I should. "I'm stuck in this villa with my target, who practically sleeps naked every night. My back still hasn't recovered from sleeping on a hard loveseat. I'm *never* going to a couples thera—relationship coach ever again. Right now, I'm the middle of some type of *Mean Girls* feud. Worst of all, I'm competing in an Olympic tournament that considers furniture assembly a sport."

"I'm impressed you've survived being around someone that pretentious this long, and I'm a little jealous of the fun activities."

There's no point in bringing up kissing Basil since it has no bearing on the client updates. That, and I've decided to keep my distance from now on. "She's not bad once you get to know her. Complex, but there's a heart inside her chest." I change the subject before oversharing. "It's impossible to not fall in love with this gorgeous island."

"Don't tell Nikita, but since we didn't have a honeymoon, I'm trying to surprise her with a trip to Sapphire Isle. It also gives us a chance to check out Bangkok for a few nights. Too bad the waitlist is over eighteen months now."

I tilt my head. "Is that why you wanted me to take this case, conning me with a vacation? One that conveniently involves the owners of the resort?"

"No, I *encouraged* you to take a stress-free vacation, which I'm starting to believe isn't possible. You meeting the owners was a complete coincidence. I provided you with a change of scenery. Even your car told me it was sick of your company." She laughs. "The money is incredible, as will be my ten percent differential for the overtime I've put in. Thank you for that in advance, by the way."

"You're lucky the food here is amazing." I recall Kaydence and Nikita discussing opting out of a wedding reception and fancy vacation to save money for purchasing their house. Given this client's level of exacting standards, she deserves every dime, and she and Nikita deserve the best honeymoon. "You two would love it here. "

I peer out at the endless water, taking in the smell of

clean air while silence spreads between us. When I return to the camera, her eyes are down as if she's in deep thought. "There's something I need to talk to you about."

"Something wrong? Is everyone okay?"

"Yeah. Everyone's safe and fine. I've been thinking a lot about how to say this." Her eyes meet mine. "I need you to take over client communications."

I blink and breathe a sigh of relief that nothing awful has happened. We've already talked about her taking time off. Maybe she forgot? "Of course. With the baby coming, you're good to take a step back from some future reports."

Her eyes point toward the ground again. "Not some, *all* reports." She exhales. "Starting with this case."

There's a sinking feeling in my stomach. "Oh."

"I get that you don't speak directly to clients after the Grace situation. You fell for a narcissist who took advantage of your heart. I respect your decisions, and I'm really sorry to put this on you at the last minute, but I haven't been honest with myself. We're not just colleagues. You're my best friend, King."

"Anything you need, I'm here."

"I'm burning out. Fast. With Rosie and after all the attempts for our second child, the IVF journey has taken a toll on us. Nikita and I have been working hard trying to support each other, but I need to quit this in order to be there for her. Plus, this client is high maintenance."

I push the sting of rejection away. This isn't about my feelings right now. I listen and offer reassurance for the next several minutes. She has been holding a lot in. Mamma told me it was my eyes—the type people want to tell anything to. I understood because I always felt the same about hers. She had such kind, caring eyes. Although I had no reason to be concerned about acceptance when I came out, I appreciated those same eyes as I told her I wanted to go to prom with a girl.

Tuning back in, I settle into a deck chair, anticipating Kaydence's usual bouncing between topics. She jumps from work stress to marriage to what she's cooking for this year's Friendgiving. She rambles on about everything, including offering advice on my life.

"And don't carry on being afraid to get close to anyone," she commands, a declaration in her voice. "Not every woman is going to stab you in the back. Life happens, and oftentimes we come out stronger in the end. Irony aside, try giving yourself a little grace. We all have to learn how to trust ourselves."

I huff. "Right. That's why I put rules in place for myself." I leave out the part where I broke one by mixing work with pleasure. Never again.

"Here I am breaking your biggest rule: always finish a case. I used to hate the thought of quitting anything, but you know what? I can't let pride win. I need to get back to what truly makes me happy: being a wife, mom, and cyber security genius—and playing matchmaker for you."

I know she's right about letting people in, but it feels nearly impossible sometimes. Basil comes to mind, and so does the added layer of complication that is my attraction to her.

"I have to get some sleep. I'll give the client your number," Kaydence says. "Luckily, I managed to talk her down on some of her demands for the remaining case updates, but she's deadly serious about having a close eye on Jones, and you know what? I get it now. Anyway, talk later."

When the call ends, I return inside the villa and see Basil bent over, peering inside the refrigerator. A rose-colored bikini paints her skin underneath a sheer cover-up. Before she catches me checking her out, I pull my eyes away and go change into my swimsuit.

Now that I'm taking on client communication, I need greater caution than before. I try not to think about what might happen if Basil finds out I've been surveilling her. I've been around her long enough to know she'd be upset. No amount of beach dates would refute that reality. If getting close to her benefits the case, so be it. Otherwise, she's off-limits. *We're* off-limits.

Basil and I walk toward the beach in a comfortable silence until we stop at a cozy corner semi-blocked-off by towering rocks not far from the shore. Both our jaws drop. There's a table set up for two, in the center of rose petals in the shape of a heart on the sand.

Minutes later, we're seated and served by a private chef, our smiles as full as our glasses of chardonnay. There's enough wine, salad, and shrimp scampi to feed five, which the chef advised they'd package for us and have delivered to our villa that afternoon.

For dessert, we lay out on a beige blanket and relax. I catch peeks of Basil's smooth tan legs between bites from the mini dessert bar provided. Even though we both had full stomachs, we couldn't deny the decadence. Despite the high sun, there's a slight breeze, cool enough to keep the food and us from melting in the heat, but not warm enough to dare me to swim. To be fair, entering the water isn't on my agenda, even if wearing my swim shorts and black bikini is. Basil, on the other hand, has already hinted at taking a swim together twice since we began eating. She catches the end of my longest glance and rests her sunglasses on top of her head, a toothy grin on her face.

"This isn't so bad." She motions a hand through the air. "A secret hiding spot. Food. Drinks. Peace and quiet. I don't think even Lynn and Mae could find us."

"Be careful what you wish for." I let out a small chuckle, imagining Lynn barreling in. Then I contemplate the question on my mind. I take a sip of wine. "Can I ask you something?"

"Shoot," she replies, applying sunscreen lotion to her arms. "What are you thinking about?"

"You and Victoria? Did you two used to date, or...?"

"Oh, god, no." Basil's mouth forms into a displeased pout, and she takes a more curt tone. "Short or long version?"

"Whichever."

The way her nose wrinkles tells me there is no short version. I casually add space between us, leaning back and resting on my elbows. She seems to notice but doesn't comment.

"She had a fling with my sister back when we were in high school. People found out and Victoria, being the coward she is, twisted the story into something it wasn't. It was so unbelievable and..." Basil pauses and regroups. This appears to be a touchy subject. "Let's just say it turned into a nightmare at home and with the school board, which both Victoria and our mothers were on."

I pull my eyebrows together. "How did the school board end up responding?"

Basil scoffs. "I buried Victoria's reputation before they got a chance. It wasn't like I didn't give her an opportunity to make the situation right. She chose her path, and so did I. It led me to start my first business. An anti-bullying nonprofit. As class president, I ran a fundraiser at school. Raised enough money for a billboard, and guess whose face was the star bully's?"

"You *didn't*."

"Oh, I did. You know, people really underestimate the work that goes into fundraising."

That was an unconventional, yet effective route to revenge. "That's quite a way to make her never forget."

"I'm not entirely soulless. I was one hundred percent transparent with my plans if she refused to rectify the situation. Causing violence toward someone else because you're afraid of what others will think of you is intolerable."

I nod in agreement.

She tosses me the sunscreen lotion bottle. "She hurt my sister. Of course I was protective. Our parents had divorced six months prior. Rumors were flying about our family, and I'm not one for standing around doing nothing. Feeling helpless doesn't sit well with me. Should I have handled it differently? Maybe, maybe not; but I created a plan and executed it. Reputation matters to me." She exhales deeply. "After trusting my heart to the wrong person, I guess I should add loyalty and integrity to the list."

I nod my head and cross one leg over the other. Me too. "That's understandable."

"I felt guilty about the fundraiser, but then I started to receive messages from people sharing their stories and how I had helped them, so I created an organization that's expanded over the years, helping thousands to cope and learn to live authentically. Some risks are worth taking."

She goes quiet, seeming lost in thought, her gaze is planted on a buoy floating ahead. After a long stretch of sounds of rolling waves and birds, she downs her remaining wine and meets my eyes. "Swim with me?"

I shake my head. A playful smile paints my lips, but she doesn't seem as amused, only tilting her head in disbelief. "That was not a part of our agreement."

"Neither is the way you keep looking at me. But here we are."

"Right." I pick up my aviator sunglasses and cover my eyes. "Problem solved."

She laughs. "What on earth do you think happens when two people go on a date?"

"Is that what this is? A date?" A part of me wants to hear the words out loud.

She leans close enough to make my insides constrict and gently removes my sunglasses, forcing our eyes to hold.

Her eyes travel to my lips and back up. Her voice is barely audible. "Yes."

When she drifts closer, I sense her fingers near mine. It's nearly impossible, but somehow, I stop myself from kissing her and face the water. "Lucky for you, I'm not much of an ocean person. Feel free to enjoy yourself though."

She exhales at the rejection and backs away; same with her fingers. "Not a fan of swimming?"

"I don't care for swimming with other animals. You know it's their territory, not ours."

"You're afraid of fish," she says in a deadpan manner.

"That's not what I said."

She raises her brow in the way she does when challenged, then she stands, legs hovering near my face, and shimmies her shoulders until her cover-up falls to the ground. "You'll know where I'll be if you care to join."

I trail every step she takes toward the water. As if knowing I'm watching, she runs her fingers underneath the sides of her bikini bottoms and throws a casual smile over her shoulder, then enters the water.

Five minutes later, the blazing sun beams on my body, and I wipe the sweat from my temples. Sighing, I give into temptation and join Basil. For the case.

We linger where our feet can still reach the rocky bottom. The sunlight reflects off the water, detailing the textures of gray and black rocks. There are tiny fish, but I try to dismiss them, unlike Basil, who offers me a victorious grin when she sees me. It's hard to ignore the effect her big dimpled-grin has on me. When the distance closes between us, the fluttering sensation deep in my chest returns. Taking two hands, I playfully splash her. She returns the favor, slamming the water, and jolts away. I chase her.

The distance between us slowly dissolves with each minute. Our playful touches grow into teasing hands on skin. Any worry about the case vanishes as we exchange giggles. Another joy-filled day, another moment the world melts away, only us remaining.

Basil emerges from underneath the water, then fixes her gaze on me, her damp brown hair dripping down her shoulders. She feels something too, doesn't she?

My question is soon answered as smooth legs brush against mine. I don't pull away. My thudding heart forces me forward, both hands sliding down Basil's sides. The coolness of the water is now in contact with the wetness building between my thighs as Basil's legs tighten around my waist. We don't speak, letting our bodies do the talking. Not breaking eye contact, I maneuver my hands underneath Basil's ass and prop her up until her full breasts press against me. Suddenly, my fear of what's swimming in this ocean with me is the least of my problems.

Our mouths remain inches apart. The way she whispers my name makes my skin goosebump and my planted stance nearly collapse. Sensing her lips within reach, I close my eyes and lean in, unable to stop myself.

"Ouch! Damn it!" I yelp and writhe, bucking my hips forward, and launch Basil backward until her back slaps the water with a volume that makes me cringe. Searing fire zips up my leg. My eyes well up as I grimace from the tormenting pain flooding over me.

"What?" Basil yells in concern. She waves her arms, searching the water for the culprit. She asks again after I answer only with a string of expletives. "Slow down. What's wrong?"

Not seeing anything either, I pause. Our eyes meet, and my face sinks. "Everything."

Without another word I swim to shore, leaving Basil and our ruined moment behind.

* * *

"Can I see it?" Basil asks for the second time.

"No," I mutter. A hiss of pain falls from my lips from the burning streaks of agony. I typically process pain alone, which is clearly the opposite of her plans. Sitting spread-eagle on top of a counter in a public restroom while my target examines my crotch is an obvious response from the universe for my foolishness. Why can't I stay away from her?

"You may not," I insist. "There are people around. It's embarrassing."

Her raised brow reminds me of her sassiness…and how she refuses to not get what she wants. "Have it your way, then."

She takes a step back and yells as if she's making an announcement to the entire island. "I can *assure* you there is nothing embarrassing about your wife being between your legs on our honeymoon."

Giggles echo against the walls and the remaining women pass and stare. Basil returns her tone to normal when the room is empty. "There. Privacy." She smiles and locks the door. "Nothing I haven't seen before, darling. Now strip."

Eventually, I do as I'm told and cover my lap with a shirt, then carefully maneuver my boy-shorts bikini off. With legs clamped shut, I say, "I don't know what stung me, but it hurts like hell. This is your fault. I told you—"

"Quit being stubborn and let me help you." Basil's commanding tone is back as she holds my gaze.

I wish those gazes would end. Our shared looks make my stomach flutter. I take a deep breath. We're alone, which makes the situation easier to trust. My cheeks are ablaze from being naked and vulnerable, as well as the stinging sensation on my upper thigh. I reluctantly drift my legs open for Basil to study the injury.

Her face turns serious, and she bends down to examine. "Thought so. A jellyfish sting." Using two fingers, she spreads my legs wider. The grimace on her face worries me. "A nasty one. Do you feel any chest pain or difficulty swallowing?"

I inhale through my nose and let the air exit my mouth. "No…I don't think so. Maybe? Why are you asking questions like I'm dying?"

Basil's light chuckle calms me a bit. "Just procedural questions. The good news is I don't see any tentacles to remove."

My mind flurries with panic. "Tentacles?! See, this is why I don't swim in the—"

A sudden shiver travels up my spine. My fingers clench the sides of the countertop as cool air from Basil's breath caresses up and down my inner thigh. The ache I have has officially drifted north.

"Does that help?" She looks up, and the air seems to leave the room, reminding me of our failed kiss earlier. A coy smile tugs at her lips. "If not, I can try something else."

Naughty images of what "something else" looks like comes to mind.

Then I pause, and my nose scrunches. "Wait. You're not going to do what I think you are, are you? I'm not into the pee—"

"No. *That's* a myth." She rolls her eyes and jokingly swats my non-injured leg. I can tell she's starting to get irritated by me, which I admit is a bit out of character. She rises. "Let's make a quick trip to the taco bar for ice. You should be good to go for the semifinals. Keep an eye on it just in case. Doctor's orders."

"Thank you, Dr. Jones."

She sees my smile and shakes her head. "That's my sister, not me. I've always been a little jealous that she got that title. I'm glad she pursued her passion though."

"Wine isn't yours?" I ask.

"Don't get me wrong, I love my job, but sometimes I wish I had control of my career path. I'm hard on her, but honestly, Hazel's always been the brave one. Taking the path with the most resistance toward her happiness."

"Are you happy?"

Her lips form a pout. "I should be," she says matter-of-factly, then hesitates. "I knew I wanted to be my own boss at age five, and taking over the family business was the blueprint. Following in my mother's footsteps made the most sense. She's tough, but she just wants me to be the best. I used to picture myself taking care of people like my sister. Less Big Pharma, more natural methods." She fixes her gaze to the wall. "I dreamed of having my own apothecary boutique shop, but I'll have something much bigger and better if I stick to the current plan."

"It's never too late. I started my business years ago for similar reasons."

Basil's interest seems to pique. "What type of work do you do?"

"Um—consulting." I circle back to my injured leg, attempting to play it off like I wasn't throwing a childlike tantrum minutes ago. "I'm good as new. Thank you."

Basil starts to say something else but hesitates. "I'm sorry for not being honest with you back in Seattle. I wanted to prove how sorry I was today, not cause any more pain. Truth is, I'm glad you're here with me on the island." There's sincerity in her voice. She plants a tender kiss along the most sensitive area of my inner thigh.

Butterflies erupt in my stomach, accompanying a tingle between my legs, doing me no favors.

"I'll be outside when you're ready."

Once I'm alone, my heart rate returns to normal. I take my time getting dressed and gathering my belongings since no one is waiting to use the restroom. Pretending to be a happy couple reminds me of what I don't have, what I won't let myself have. Over the years, I've refused to fall for someone, because letting yourself fall in love means giving away a piece of your puzzle-shaped heart, and how can I when there are so few pieces left?

Why am I entertaining the idea of being with anyone, let alone Basil? She was just left at the altar. I'm probably nothing more than a rebound. Then there's the case.

Maybe Basil and I were doomed from the start, but I can't deny my feelings for her. Being on this island is beyond messy, and yet I don't want it to end.

I retrieve my phone from my bag and check the screen. Three missed calls in the last thirty minutes—the case.

When the device lights up again, I think about ignoring it. After a deep exhale, I press the answer button. "King speaking." My insides constrict hearing the words on the other end. I take a final glance at the closed door before responding to the woman. "Yes, Ms. Jones, I have an update on your daughter."

CHAPTER 16

BASIL

"THE STARS ARE NICE," I say, on my side of the pillow wall, peering through the ceiling's skylight window. I hate small talk, but the tension—and not the sexy kind—between Caroline and me is painfully apparent. I can't tell what time it is, but I know it's past midnight, and falling asleep seems like an impossible task. My mind has been preoccupied with thoughts of her, and if it's somehow possible, I've been thinking about her *more* since our massage and beach date today. One minute, she's reaching for me, showering me with passionate kisses, and the next she seems distant. Why the change? What did I do? My brain is going through gymnastics attempting to figure this out. Innately, I'm a problem solver, and I can't help but wonder if something needs to be fixed.

"Today was fun. Thank you." She ends the growing awkward silence. "I mean that."

My heart warms, happy to hear it given the unfolding of today's events. "How's your leg?"

"Better."

Maybe if I say the words out loud, I'll be able to stop

craving her touch. I lift the pillow next to our heads and take in her silhouette from the light illuminating from above. "Is something bothering you?"

"Yes." She doesn't look at me. "But I'll be fine. It's nothing you did wrong."

At least she appears to be honest. "Okay...good night. Don't let the jellyfish bite."

I catch a glimpse of her slight smile as she pulls the pillow from my grip and returns the figurative brick back in place. She feels miles away. I return staring at the stars. Based on her breathing, I can tell she's not privy to sleep either.

More silence.

How could anyone stand this? It's unproductive and excruciating. I shift my approach. Maybe meditation will help both of us. "Do you want to do the breathing exercise?"

She lifts the same pillow from before and faces me. "Now? At 2 a.m.?"

I wrestle out from underneath the sheets and walk around the bed, then stop on the rug. With my back facing her, I plop down and cross one leg underneath the other. "Yes."

"Want a pillow to sleep down there? Someone needs to be able to function at the tournament and gala tomorrow."

Sleep on the floor? *"Seriously?"* We're taking steps backward now? I yank around to discover a smirk and relax when I realize she isn't serious. "I'm the one who made sure we weren't late to any of the events." Even 1 a.m. game night, Battle of the Sapphics. Caroline wasn't fond of being up that late. "We're not missing that gala. You will survive being awake for seven more minutes."

I turn back around and stare at the door. Sounds of ocean waves distract my mind while I wait. A couple of minutes later, she's out of bed, and then I hear footsteps. When her back touches mine, I smile, appreciating the sense of calm, and remember how good her warmth felt inside Lady Shiba's office.

We don't set a timer. A few minutes later, a part of me is glad I forgot. Turns out I needed this too. As our breathing synchronizes, the tension between us melts away.

Eventually, I speak up. "It's not like we're going to see each other ever again, if you want to talk about anything." Saying that last part stings more than I expected.

Silence.

I guess I'll lead by example. Deep breath. "I was left at the altar, and I think it was my fault…and the worst part is…" I pause. "I went on my honeymoon in hopes of saving my chances at a promotion. Pretty awful, aren't I?"

"No."

"Then there's the fact that being here with you is some of the most fun I've had with anyone, and that's scary and also frustrating. Since meeting you, it feels like everything I believe in is being challenged." I swallow the lump forming in my throat. Her steady breathing is the only thing preventing me from falling apart. "We've known each other less than three weeks, and I feel like you're one of the few trustworthy people I know."

Her shoulder muscles slump against mine. "Please don't say that. You don't know me, Basil." I feel the rhythm of her breath change.

"But that's the thing. I want to. If you'll let me."

She shakes her head. "I don't know if that's possible. Plus, I don't want to start anything I can't finish. I've been hurt before too."

"What happened?" I whisper into the void. I'm met with more silence. Maybe asking wasn't a good idea.

"I risked my career to be with someone, and…" She huffs. "I realized too late that she never planned to choose me.

Everything between us was a lie from the start. For her it was."

"I'm sorry."

"Me too. I'm afraid I'll make the same mistake again. Maybe we both aren't good in the relationship department."

We share a hollow laugh. Then I ask a question, catching myself by surprise. "What do you think our marriage would look like if it were real? I mean, I know this is fake. Just curious. I'll start: you're on spider duty."

Feeling her body move as she laughs makes my lips turn upward. "Didn't you catch line thirteen in our marriage contract?" Using her free hand, she swipes the open air. "Both parties must alternate spider duties every three years."

"I guess that's what a cat is for."

"I didn't think you were the animal type."

"I'm not." I chuckle. "But we all have to compromise sometimes." That's something I'd never thought I'd say.

"Where would we live?" she asks. "Hypothetically."

"I don't know. I'm open to moving from Seattle."

She nods in agreement. "We could have a business—" She changes her voice to an infomercial: "'King's Apothecary. You've got a scratch, we've got your back.'"

I crack up laughing. "You're ridiculous."

"Or..." Caroline continues, "'King's Apothecary: Famous for soaps, oils and everything Basil.' It's street-side so customers can see our Sapphic Olympics trophy. If we win."

"When we win," I correct her. Dropping out of the tournament is officially not happening.

"Outside of bragging rights, the brochure said winners get a trophy and free trip back to the island. The top three teams receive some type of 'SM Box.' Not sure what that is. Sapphire Merchandise? Sapphic Magic? All I remember is a picture of a black box with a red bow on it. There's only one way to find out for sure."

"Win," I whisper. Victoria's words in my head attempt to ruin the moment, but I don't let them. "That all sounds nice." It's not my reality, but I'm enjoying thoughts of creating my own life blueprint for a change.

Our conversation continues, and we lose track of time. I tell her what it was like for me to grow up with a twin. I adore every second of hearing about Caroline's genuine joy in being a godmother.

Some time later, she laughs. "I think we surpassed seven minutes. Lady Shiba would be proud."

I don't bother searching to see what time it is. "We probably should go to bed soon." I turn my body to face her. She twists around, and we pause as if simultaneously remembering what's supposed to happen next.

Her gaze drifts to my lips and back up. "After this..." Her hand finds the side of my face. She gently kisses me, and the butterflies in my stomach flutter at the tenderness of her touch.

I deepen the kiss, knowing seven seconds have come and gone. I break away, just barely. "I like this part very much," I whisper against her lips.

"Me too." She brushes our lips together, then rests her forehead against mine and lets out an exhale. "Me too."

CHAPTER 17

CAROLINE

THE GALA IS MORE exquisite than I imagined. I scan the room while I wait for Basil. Crystal chandeliers hang from the ceiling, illuminating the sea of guests with a warm glow. The atmosphere has been a mixture of allure, elegance, and desire, from the double-door entrance, to the stage where the burlesque dancers are performing. Queer women, varying in sizes and skin tones and all dressed to the nines, are chatting, eating, and dancing as joy fills the air. The room smells of white tea and the summation of the delicate flower centerpieces at each round table.

"Caroline, your wife is *absolutely* stunning. I simply adore that gown on her," Mae tells me, seated two chairs down, as Basil re-enters the ballroom after freshening up.

For the first time in a long while, I'm speechless. Although we arrived together, there's something about seeing her from afar that reminds me of the way our eyes met back in Seattle. It wasn't long after that our lips were introduced to each other.

Unable to focus on anything else—not the case, not the Olympics, not the live jazz or Mae adjusting Lynn's bow tie for the fourth time. My gaze locks on Basil. Murmurs of conversation vanish as she approaches, her heels clicking against the marble floor. Her wide lipstick grin finds me, and I wonder what she's thinking about. Her off-shoulder navy-blue satin gown hugs her curves just right. Lips parted, I scan up the thigh slit of her dress, which shows off the tan she's been working hard to achieve. Her hair is elegantly draped on one side, loose waves teasing the bare parts of her shoulder. She's beautiful, hips swaying with each heeled step, a confidence in her that I hadn't noticed before.

"You look gorgeous," I tell her as if it's my first time seeing her this evening. Back inside the villa, the words crossed my mind, but I didn't say them out loud then.

A soft hand rests in my lap after she sits next to me. "Thank you. You don't clean up too bad yourself."

Our eyes hold. "Thanks."

She twists inward a little more. "I'm impressed with your outfit. Not many people can pull off suspenders without looking dorky." Returning to her original position, she casually points her gaze across from her in Lauren's direction.

Underneath the table, I caress the top of her fingers with mine as I lean closer and find her ear. "Be nice."

"I *am*. It's not like I said it to her face." Her eye twitches when I give her a look. "Fine. I'll be nice."

Like clockwork, Victoria seems to sense our conversation about them and flashes a glare. Thankfully, Lynn speaks up before either of them lose their composure.

"Looks like Mae and I aren't the only ones celebrating tonight." Lynn's face lights up, and she squeezes her wife's hand, then raises her glass of champagne. "Thanks to both of your teams winning earlier today, we will have the fiercest women participating in the championship. I always say friendly competition is one thing that brings people from different backgrounds together. That's why I launched the

Sapphic Olympics. Watching the matches today, I don't regret it for a second. Cheers to good fun, no matter what happens." We toast. "I told Mae this year's tournament would be the best one yet."

"Certainly appears that way," Mae says. She directs her attention to Victoria and Lauren. "Perhaps we can start ramping up awareness. I wouldn't know where to start with social media, and if I left it up to Lynn, all we'd see are pictures of food, boobs, and beer, like this is some type of lesbian sorority."

"And Quilliam." Smiling, Lynn lifts her hands in defense at her wife's raised brow. We all laugh.

"Yes, Mrs. Blakeman," Lauren says. "We have a meeting with our social media team booked next week. We understand you're busy. The good news is that you can manage as little or as much of each account as you prefer."

Mae's face lights up. "That is lovely to hear."

Victoria nods. "It's also our job to protect clients from any potentially poor business queries or bad press, which is why PR can be so crucial." She glances at me suspiciously, then shifts to face Basil with a devious curl in her lips. "That'd be about as bad as being left at the altar."

Thankfully, Basil doesn't leap out her chair and start a WWE match in the middle of this gala.

"The good news is we haven't had any negative experiences in over twenty years, and with your help, our record will continue," Mae says. "Okay, no more shop talk. I'm over my ten-minute allotment. I made Lynn a promise."

Basil is attempting to smile, despite having that streak of red on her neck. She's *not* happy.

The music's tempo slows, sedating the dance floor as couples gently sway to the calming rhythm. Mae stands, her hand intertwined with Lynn's, and slowly pulls her wife out of the chair.

Lynn laughs, kissing Mae's fingers, and points at me and Basil. "I'll go if they go."

I straighten my back and search for Basil's eyes. I'm not a fan of dancing, but at this point, I'd do anything to get her and Victoria away from each other. "Let's go."

She nods and stands. Relieved to get a break from being in the middle of the feud, I do the same and welcome her fingers pushing through mine. We follow the Blakemans to the dimly lit dance floor. The weight of Basil's arm wrapping around my shoulder cues me to gently grab her hand and sway.

"Thank you for getting me away. I can't wait to rub the first-place trophy right in her face."

"I bet."

I pull her tighter, and I catch a whiff of the same intoxicating perfume she wore when we first met. Suddenly aware of our closeness, my heart rate jumps. I almost step on her dress, but catch myself. "Sorry."

She laughs at my little side step dance. "Is that nervousness I sense? How unlike you." She pulls back slightly. Her dimple peeks out as her cheeks lifts. "I hope you weren't this clumsy when you danced at prom."

I meet her eyes. "Actually, I didn't go to prom."

"Not once?"

"Nope. I asked a girl senior year. I had a crush on her for months and I heard she had a thing for me, so I went for it. My mom gave me a great idea for the whole big proposal. I asked when we were walking to school one morning. She declined. She said she 'didn't believe in that.' I didn't bother asking anyone else."

Basil frowns. "That sounds like something right out of a horror movie. I'm sorry. Was she out?"

"I thought so. Maybe not. I was naive about a lot of things back then." Basil's so easy to talk to when we're alone. "Every once in a while, I wish I had gone to prom instead of crying all night. Well, until my dad filled the house with his Prince album and made me dance with him." I chuckle at the memory of James and I belting 80's hits. "That's what happens when your dad is a choreographer."

"I thought you said that your father was a military man?"

I hesitate. This is what happens when I'm not careful. I guess I can tell her the truth.

"He is. I also have a dad who is a 'world class choreographer.' His words, not mine."

"Two dads. Got it." Basil pauses our footsteps. "And your mother?"

"She passed a long time ago. My parents are polyamorous. My mom was bisexual—same for dad. James has been my dad's current partner since I was my early school years." For some reason, I start to ramble explaining their relationship structure, then reign myself back in. "I've learned the look people give when their heads start to spin. Basil's almost at that point.

"Do you call them both dad?" She seems genuinely curious, not in a judgmental way, which I appreciate.

"Sometimes. Usually I'll call one dad and the other by his first name. James."

"Was it complicated growing up?"

"Eh, I felt safer inside my house than at some other kids' because their parents were asses. I had a great childhood. It got much easier once we settled after my dad retired from the military. He decided shortly after my mother passed."

"I'm sorry for your loss. And for all the questions. I've never met anyone with poly parents before."

"Don't be. I understand it can be difficult to understand if you're not familiar with it. And thank you." I offer a half smile. "She's always with me."

Basil rests her head on my shoulder and we continue

swaying in a comfortable silence. "I went to prom three times and none was as good as dancing with you." She smiles. "You didn't miss much, I promise."

My cheeks warm and I can't help but laugh at her compliment. "*Now* I am nervous."

"Why?"

"I don't know. Maybe you just have that effect on me."

"And what effect is that?"

"Making me forget how to breathe." I didn't mean for the words to leave my mind, but it's too late now.

Her eyes crinkle at the corners, sparkling with a mix of mischief and flirtation, an irresistible combination she knows I can't refuse. "What makes you think you're the only one feeling that way right now?"

Instead of separating when the next song begins, we continue slow dancing. She gravitates toward me, and when her chin tilts, I press my lips against hers.

CHAPTER 18

BASIL

THE ALREADY OVERWHELMING charge between Caroline and me skyrocketed the moment we stepped inside the villa. By the time I realized the boldness of my actions, it was too late. I crash our lips together, slamming her spine against the door, like she did to me days ago, kissing her with an appetite I didn't know I had. Her grip on my thighs tighten, and the needy touch of her lips canvassing the sensitive parts of my neck drives me wild.

"Bedroom," I mutter between kisses, barely catching my breath while kicking off my heels. "Actually, do whatever you want to me, and I don't care where."

With a mischievous grin, she twists me around, firmly pinning our bodies together. Soft lips brush the back of my neck, sending tiny tremors down my spine. "I want you in my mouth, *now*," she growls against my skin, ruining my panties in the process. A faint scent of coconut and vanilla from her hair fills my nose, pulling me deeper into my already sexually intoxicated state. She grabs my hand and leads us toward the bed. "Soundproofing might come in handy after all."

My brain scrambles to prepare for a night I already know will be more intense than the first time. My dress demands removal, but then I remember how Caroline's hot and heavy desire transformed into what felt like hours of teasing. Given the way she's staring at me, her carnivorous gaze on mine gives me hope I won't have to wait long.

We don't waste time unbuttoning her shirt or removing my dress, yet it doesn't seem fast enough. Next thing I know, her lips, her tongue, her hands engulf me. Hungry kisses travel down my neck and shoulder, then clavicle, increasing the jolts of pleasure between my thighs. Every inch of me is pulsing. My heart pounds when she takes off the rest of her clothes. With hooded eyes, I devour her naked body up and down as she approaches and gently pushes me onto the bed.

Both of my hands are pinned underneath Caroline's firm grip. She commands me not to move.

"You should see how hot you look right now," she whispers in my ear.

I breathe and find her mouth again. "Make me yours."

We break for air and she pauses briefly to meet my eyes. "Don't worry. I'm going to fuck you like I own you." Her hand glides down the center of my body, caressing my soft inner thighs en route to her destination. She slips underneath my panty line, and when she feels my wetness, we both hiss.

"Fuck." The word comes out in a breathy moan. Her hand retracts. "I missed how good you feel."

Our mouths lock again, and I get lost in the warmth of her skin engulfing mine. I love how wet she makes me. With her irises as dark as my black lace bra, Caroline trails up the valley of my breasts with her tongue, never taking her eyes off mine. She puts her mouth over the fabric covering my nipple, and the heated sensation of her breath blended with the delicate lace patterns pressing into my skin overwhelms me. She teases for a moment longer, flicking her tongue over the hardening bud until she's satisfied, then repeats on the other side. I wish I was fully naked, but I don't dare move my hands from above my head, knowing she might drag this sensual torture out longer if I so much as twitch.

As if reading my mind, Caroline motions for me to remove my bra, which I do at a rapid speed. My back arches as she trails a path of light kisses down my body while a hand kneads my breast. Then she slowly slides my panties down my legs and tosses them onto the floor.

I can smell my slickness when she spreads my knees and positions herself between them. My fingers grip the sheets tighter at the flicks of her tongue teasing the space between my inner thigh and where I want her most. My pussy lips are throbbing for her, and she knows it. She's enjoying herself, keeping my legs pinned in place as she whispers naughty words against my skin, inches from my clit.

She stops, pulls back, and watches me wiggle my hips for her attention. She lets out a small laugh, seemingly pleased with herself. "So needy."

My breathy expletives turn into a groan. *"Please—"*

Her tongue firmly strokes upward between my pussy lips, and I cry out her name, which fuels her intensity as she continues.

With complete control of the placement of my legs, she licks and laps over the tiny pebble, sending my brain into a frenzied state. Mouth still at work, two of her fingers trace circles around my entrance, making my hips grind against her lips. My eyes roll back as she slowly enters me, exploring every inch of my walls.

Her rhythm increases, and she fucks me with deeper, more determined strokes, curling her fingers in all the right spots. My muscles constrict around her. My moans paint the walls as she sucks my clit and thrusts into me.

Climax brews in the pit of my belly. Small waves build into an earth-crashing rush with each thrust. This feels so much better than our first night together, something I didn't think was possible.

Her delightful moans from her full mouth drive me closer to the edge. Overwhelmed by pleasure, my hips rock forcefully as she sucks harder, lapping my clit with rapid speed. The push-pull sensation weakens my knees. I let go, relinquishing Caroline's touch, and I cry out as the breaking waves of climax wash over me.

Caroline's grip relaxes as she slowly kisses my inner legs and lower stomach. My legs tremble when she flattens her tongue and slowly tastes me, coating her tongue with her handiwork.

I steady my breathing as she climbs up, and it's only then I realize she's still wearing pants. I tug at the button and slide them halfway down her hips, until our mouths demand more kisses. The taste of my desire turns me on more than before.

"Not yet." Her lips brush mine again, making the butterflies flutter uncontrollably. "I'm going to show you *exactly* what this honeymoon bed is meant for."

CHAPTER 19

CAROLINE

THE NEXT MORNING I stir awake and discover I'm in the bed alone. I sit up, peer around and spot Basil standing outside on the deck wearing a robe, a mug in her hands. I smile at our clothes scattered all over the room, same as our first night together—the floor, bench at the end of the bed and somehow, both the night stands.

The pillow wall is officially gone.

I rise to my feet and stretch, noting the delicious soreness in my muscles from last night. My phone's burning a hole in my bag and for the first time, I don't reach for it to start my day. A part of me doesn't want to go back to reality, a world where Basil is my target and what we first did and continue doing shouldn't happen. Nothing about last night feels wrong, quite the opposite. Instead of checking for any missed calls, I slip a Terry Cloth robe over my naked body and join Basil outside.

The sound of the sliding doors opening makes her turn. The sight of her toothy grin warms my entire being.

"Good morning." Behind her, I wrap my arms around her waist, enjoying the way she sinks into me.

"Morning." She turns her head and I place a soft kiss on her temple. "Sorry, I wanted to catch the end of the sunrise."

I immerse myself into the breathtaking blend of hazy scarlet and fiery yellow over the tranquil water. "It's gorgeous. I don't blame you." *But not as beautiful as you,* I want to say, but hold back.

We stay like this for several minutes as we rehash last night's Gala—the extravagant decorations, how much fun Lynn and Mae seemed to have had and the events that transpired between us later that night.

"I have a confession to make." Basil brings her cup to her lips and takes a sip.

A hint of cardamom from her tea teases my nose. "Hmm?"

Her cheeks color with a faint blush as she nods in a direction to the left. "I thought about your tongue while I um… pleasured myself on that deck chair one morning. You were out for a run."

"Oh, *really?*" My brows raise with my intrigue. "Well, I hope I was of exceptional service. Did you enjoy yourself?"

"Very much." She chuckles with a shy smile. "Though the real thing is a *thousand* times better."

Picturing Basil's hands at work stokes the coals inside my belly. She tries to change the subject to breakfast, but I'm not finished with the topic.

"Are you going to tell me details or leave me hanging after dropping news like *that?*" My lips find her neck. "We both know I can be quite persuasive regarding your pleasure."

She tilts her head, granting me wider access, and smiles while biting her bottom lip. "Maybe you should make me."

"Tempting." Butterflies swarm in my belly when she brings my fingers to her lips and plants a gentle kiss on them. Then an idea comes to mind. Taking my hand, I slip underneath her robe and massage her left breast. Her shallow moans fuels me to trail the tip of my tongue up the side of her neck. I appreciate the warmer weather settling in for what I plan to do next.

I carefully remove the mug from her hands, set it on the side table and return my focus to my previous activity. Her hardening nipple rolls against my palm as I'm kneading, sending waves of pleasure down my spine. I pinch the bud, gentle at first, but I can't help but squeeze harder. She hisses and groans my name, arching her back for more.

I locate her robe string and slowly pull, inch by inch, and when she realizes the robe is loosening, she squirms and grabs the fabric to cover herself.

"Uh uh," I say.

The corner of her lips tug into a smile and she drops her hands to her sides. "What are you plotting back there?"

"You wanted to watch the sunrise..." I lean closer to her ear and lower my voice. "So, pay attention and *watch* the sunrise."

I slide the robe off her shoulders and pause when she asks a question.

"What if someone sees us?"

More like hears us. "Is that a risk you're willing to take?" I nibble and drag my lips over her shoulder. Her pulse jolts underneath my skin.

She lets out a breathy moan. "Yes."

The robe hits the ground.

I drink her in. Her curves, the smoothness of her back, her freckles sprinkled on her arms. I cup her breasts, wishing they were in my mouth, and knead the fullness once more. "You're so fucking beautiful." I press my lips to her nape while my hands continue their exploration of her bare body, trailing my fingers up her sides and abdomen. "I'll guide you, if you'd like."

She nods, pressing her back against my chest. Her warm

skin on mine is driving me wild already. "You have my full attention."

"Good." The throbbing between my legs increases almost uncontrollably.

Touching the softness of her skin resting on mine overwhelms each of my senses. I want her right here. Right now. On this deck. Barely touching, I trail the tip of my tongue up her spine, engulfed in the vibrations of her moans as I tease her.

"Now, start rubbing your clit. Slowly."

She does as she's told and slips a hand between her thighs. Within seconds, I can feel the shift in her breathing against me, her body rocking as she continues to rub. I'm tempted to turn her around to face me and fuck her hard against the railing. Instead, I revel in the scent of the ocean breeze blended with her wetness and enjoy the show. I pivot my attention south after she slips a finger inside on command and thrusts into herself.

"Harder," I growl, giving her ass a little smack. She gasps and speeds up, but I want more. I run my fingers through her hair and yank her head back. "I said, fuck yourself harder."

Her breathing turns ragged as her strokes triple in speed. I can tell she's struggling to keep quiet. She must be getting close. Gasping, gripping the back of my head while using me for full support. This is the couples breathing exercise I didn't know I needed in my life. The intensity of her strokes matches her rhythm now. She doesn't know how hot this is for me, the wetness building between my legs. The need to wrap my arm around her and finish the job overwhelms me, but I'll save that for later. Right now, I love this position that we're in. The bass of her moans fuels me to whisper all the dirty things I've fantasized about doing to her since our first night together back in Seattle.

"Caroline," she pants my name. "I'm coming—"

Her hips buck and she dips her head back into my shoulder, letting out a silent scream as she soars past the edge of climax.

I hold her close. My heart races with adrenaline as she trembles against me. I caress up and down and whisper how great of a job she did and then we finish watching the final minutes of the sky's transformation. I take in the intimacy of the moment.

She turns and kisses me passionately. "That's one hell of a way to watch the sunrise."

"You both are perfect." I peck her lips, completely enamored. Everything about Basil consumes me. I plant a soft kiss on her shoulder and smile at the slight saltiness of her skin lingering on my lips. "We should get ready for the championship soon." It's the only excuse I can come up to stop the spell Basil has on me. If it were up to me, we'd have a totally different agenda today. "I know you like to show up early."

She grabs my hand and leads us toward the bedroom, leaving the robe behind. "Come on. First, we're going to need a warm up round of horizontal exercise."

CHAPTER 20

BASIL

THIS AFTERNOON IS the final round of the Sapphic Olympics. The championship. Three teams remain, and by taking one look at the two-seater kayaks resting on the beach, I know Caroline and I will win first place—utterly destroying Victoria. Lauren's collateral damage. I won't bother investing time considering the third couple. The announcer said one was a celebrity I hadn't heard of before. It seems rude, but they're irrelevant with the Bellini Babes being the team to beat. As much as I'd love to believe this competition is about gaining bonus points with the Blakemans or my disdain for losing, it's not. *This* is for Hazel. I'm determined for us to be Sapphic Olympic champions before happy hour at the Tiki Taco starts.

After the announcer finishes explaining rules and safety tips, I block the sun from my eyes and peer toward the ocean, approximating the distance we have to race. Paddle to the beacon and back to the shore, then sprint through the finish line. Seems simple enough, except I wish the waves weren't so choppy. The water has been perfect until today. As I continue my assessment, Caroline runs to meet Lynn's fist bump on the sidelines. I'd join, but the weather permits Quilliam to be here as well, and I'm not quite ready for another close encounter with a hedgehog. No matter how "happy" he is.

"I don't have experience with tandem kayaking, but I was a two-time rowing champion in college," I say when Caroline returns to my side. The water isn't exactly calm today, but I'm hopeful our combined skills—including her last-minute YouTube video binge on kayaking—will suffice.

"I'm not surprised. You seem good at everything you put your hands on."

Her warm smile snaps me from my serious demeanor. I face her, and a flirtatious grin crosses my face as I step closer. "Including you?"

She wraps her arms around my waist and pulls me close, as if we're alone, not surrounded by hundreds of people. "Especially me."

Like we're an actual married couple, I peck her lips. "Ready to use those strong muscles of yours to steer us to victory?"

Caroline nods. "I have a feeling I'm going to need another massage after this."

"You might not know this about me, but I took a massage class. I'd love to practice my skills later. For as long as it takes." This is the type of people-pleasing I can support.

She chuckles, her gaze lands on my lips, and our eyes meet. "Careful. I will test that theory to its breaking point. Win or lose."

I ignore the last part; instead, my mind jumps to our makeout session during the massage class and dirty thoughts of what could've happened if time had permitted. After this event, time will be on my side.

Maybe I don't want this to end after we leave the island. "I'm counting on it."

We slip our life jackets on and stand next to our yellow kayak, ready for the whistle. I sense Caroline staring at me from behind and turn. Am I forgetting something? "What?"

Her beautiful grin beams, relaxing my shoulders. "I was just thinking I have the best view in the house."

The heat in my cheeks travels to my ears as I match her smile. I bet I'm blushing the same shade of red as my bikini. I love the way she always takes me by surprise. Her ability to derail my thoughts—for good or evil—is a profound mystery to me. No one else in my life has been this distracting in all the right ways.

Once our moment is over, I shift my focus to my right toward the Bellini Babes and try not to roll my eyes at their matching hot-pink tank tops and kayak. As well as their, as Lynn puts it, "peachy-cool" couple handshake. They do appear genuinely happy together. Good for them. Before they notice me watching, I return my attention forward.

Paddle in hand, I slide my sunglasses over my eyes and locate the beacon once more, ready to win with Caroline by my side. Ready to destroy Victoria Miller. Ready to prove myself to my mother. *Look alive, Basil.*

The whistle sounds. All three couples lunge toward the water, rushing to be seated, and push off the kayaks. Splashing and cheers erupt all around us. Scents of salt and seaweed fill my nose as we steady with each stroke into an effortless rhythm. Although my heart is racing, I'm in my element. Focused. Confident. With the best Olympic partner one could ask for.

The smell of grilled food fades along with the blowing horns as we launch further from the shore. I glance back and see the blue kayak in the distance—the remnants of the third couple—and note that I was right. There's only one team to beat.

The pink kayak isn't far ahead of us. We're closing in. I hear Victoria and Lauren yelling back and forth, but I can't decipher what they're saying.

The beacon isn't far now, but I know moving in a straight line is the easy part. Rotating a dual kayak within several feet of another will be difficult. Caroline and I continue full speed ahead while the pink boat drifts outward, appearing to take a wider turn. We make up the distance, reaching within paddle length near our midpoint. The price is a sharp pivot. As if Caroline can read my mind, she performs a short, powerful stroke with the paddle, and we both shift our body weight to the edge, leaning until we've cleared the beacon.

Elated, a smile splits my lips when we pass Victoria in what feels like slow motion. We're in the lead. Barely. Pain and exhaustion etch into my shoulders and core muscles from the intensity. I'm slowing down, but I'm not giving up.

There's a loud thud. Then another. This time I feel it in my bones. I twist around and grit my teeth at Victoria. The bow of their kayak bumps into us again. Then our boats are parallel. I can hear the crowd now. We're getting closer to the finish line. I'm *not* losing.

I yell to Caroline to keep paddling. Ignoring the beads of sweat forming at my temples, I stab the side of the pink kayak, which doesn't seem to change anything except now I've poked the orange bear named Victoria. She jabs her paddle in my direction. I dodge.

Then, remembering our new team name, I joust. Our paddles clash together like swords in a fencing competition. Caroline and Lauren battle to steer. I never thought this was what my personal showdown with Victoria would eventually look like, but here we are. I stab the paddle at her boat.

"I didn't realize we were playing, 'Who can make the worst decision?'" I growl. "Congratulations, you're winning!"

"You wish you could beat us." She swings her paddle, just missing my arm.

Bullying me like you did my sister? "Don't make me create another billboard, Vicky. This time I'll add *'Sore Loser'* on your big forehead!"

"Your ex-fiancée really took out the trash when dumping you, didn't she?"

My head yanks back. *Excuse me?* My eyes form slits, and my grip tightens around my paddle. "You're the perfect example of why they say, 'Less is more.'"

Caroline keeps yelling something, but I'm too livid to hear what she's saying. I am ending this competition right *now*.

I swing. And miss.

After catching my balance from the rocking, I strike again. Her paddle flies from her hands and hits the water with a splash.

I mock a smile at Victoria's slack-jawed expression. *Bitch.*

Suddenly, my paddle gets yanked from my grip. It almost slips away, but I catch the tail end of it. I tug as hard as I can. So does she.

She already has the Blakemans. She can't have this too.

Our tug-of-war continues. Expletives are flying between us. She seems stronger than me, but I don't back down. I can only imagine what those drones in the sky are projecting on the massive screen near the finish line. Usually, I'd be embarrassed to lose my composure, but sometimes, you have to take a stand for what you believe in.

"Just let go!" Caroline repeats for the second time. At first I think she's telling me to give up, then my brain registers why. I trust her.

I let go. Victoria jolts backward, and nature takes over. The incoming wave helps flip their kayak.

Caroline stops paddling, and we scan the water to make sure they're okay. I'm not a monster; I'd consider rescuing them if needed. Seconds later, the Bellini Babes emerge.

"You and your fake wife can go to hell." Victoria groans and slams her fist against their upside-down kayak. "I don't need to tell the Blakemans. They'll see it. You two don't even look like a real couple!"

I scoff. We're beautiful together. Hell, I've had more fun with Caroline than I had with someone of seven years. Caroline's *amazing*. Sometimes I swear I'm falling in love with her —*wait*. Am I? That's not possible, is it? In less than three weeks?

I return to reality and watch the couple scramble to get back inside their kayak. I tilt my head toward Victoria as Caroline paddles us away. "Darling, your opinions are like your taste in shoes: outdated and irrelevant."

Behind us now, Victoria screeches in defeat in that annoying, tantrum way I remember after putting up the anti-bullying billboard—as if she's realizing *we're* going to be the Sapphic Olympic champions, not them. I don't hear what she's screaming because my mind is too occupied with thoughts of falling in love with the woman next to me.

An explosion of cheers and whistles yanks our attention toward the beach. My jaw drops.

The blue kayak is parked in the sand, and two women are jumping up and down, hugging.

We lost…

And yet, when I remember the sight of Victoria flying into the water, I can't help feeling like a victor.

Caroline and I reach the finish line and graciously accept the fans' appreciation for our performance. With this size of crowd packed with queer women celebrating us, it's near impossible to not keep my head held high. And I'll forever savor the memory of watching Victoria march up the shore, drenched like a mad cat getting a bath. At least she's smart enough to not make a scene in front of the Blakemans. Then again, the only thing more fascinating than her lack of self-awareness is her audacity to share it. We lock eyes briefly, then she redirects her attention to her wife. I guess we're even now.

I thank the Blakemans, who won't stop hugging the four of us. According to Mae, she had Sunny pick up Quilliam, and now Sunny is pet-sitting with her ex-girlfriend. Lynn tears up as the crowd chants that silly song Lady Shiba taught us, the one I'm finding myself singing as well. I can imagine that her happy tears aren't due to the competition or the results, but the unity of the community that creates them.

All three teams stand on the championship podium, and the announcer starts to present our rewards. While applauding the third-place team, Caroline meets my gaze with a toothy grin that's impossible to not adore. She has the most beautiful smile. Us bickering over furniture during round one seems like a lifetime ago.

It's our turn to get medals placed over our heads. Caroline slides her hand into mine and intertwines our fingers. We share a laugh, and she lifts our hands to the sky while our team name is called. *Jousting Joneses*. My stomach flutters uncontrollably from her touch combined with the joy surrounding me. I make note to give her a nice, long massage later and to come up with a memorable way to thank her.

What if whatever's between us is more than the effects of this island paradise? Maybe I *am* falling in love with Caroline King.

I don't care that we're in front of what feels like the entire island. I wrap my arms around Caroline's neck and kiss her passionately. The world fades away as her grip on my waist tightens. She deepens the kiss, sending my brain to another world. At this moment, I don't feel the pain from Seattle or from the expectation to become what someone else wants me to be. Thoughts about Victoria Miller vanish. With Caroline by my side, I *won*. It's us against the world.

For the first time, I don't feel like a spectator on my own damn honeymoon.

CHAPTER 21

CAROLINE

I'M SPENDING my lunchtime video chatting with a woman who looks and sounds like Basil—with the exception of a few aging lines, but this isn't her. Despite working for Juliette Jones for years, this is our first time being face to face. Kaydence and I's inclinations were right: Juliette doesn't seem like the type of person you want on your bad side. Her composure matches her appearance, demanding respect. She methodically pauses before speaking and talks at a slower pace than Basil does. Each time she leans forward in her chair to write something down, I catch a glimpse of a picture of her standing next to Basil, a bottle of wine in each hand and a vineyard bursting with grapes in the background. Another reminder that she's my target's mother.

Our call is taking longer than intended; thankfully, it's about to end. Basil should be returning from her meeting with the Blakemans soon. Just as I go to press the End button, Juliette speaks up. "One more thing, Ms. King."

I meet her eyes. They're a similar shade of blue, but they're cold, nothing like Basil's. "Yes, ma'am?"

"Report back if my daughter is getting cozy with anyone, so I can address it. I need her to focus on work when she returns, not an affair."

I swallow and slowly nod. *About that...* My gaze sulks downward for a beat, then I face her.

Juliette appears deep in thought. Her request seems random until she continues, "I was fond of Olivia and her family. Perhaps she and Basil can sort things out with a little assistance...which could lead to another job for you."

The words stab me in the chest. That's *not* what Basil wants. It's not what I want. I fight to push away the thoughts of Basil going back to the person she trusted and who hurt her, of losing her, and of how hypocritical I sound.

My fist clenches the fabric of my shorts in frustration. It's out of character for me to challenge a client on their personal life decisions, but I can't stop the words before they exit my mouth. "Basil is a very capable and intelligent woman. I'm sure she can determine what's best for herself, including who she loves."

Juliette's raised brow makes me pause. Silence stretches between us. I can't read her expression, but the urge to quit this case right here and now is overwhelming. I *hate* that I'm doing this to Basil, but I also know I need to tread carefully. My entire career is on the line. As is my heart.

"Ms. King." Her stern demeanor is back. "I pay you well for your private investigatory skills, *not* your counsel, especially when it comes to matters concerning my daughter. As her mother, I know what's best for my child and our family legacy."

"I'm sorry, ma'am. That was out of—"

"Please don't mistake a free trip to that island as a reason to grow familiar. I pay you to complete work. Period."

Before I get a chance to respond, her desk phone rings,

and she disappears off screen. In the corner of my eye is my silver medal from the Sapphic Olympics on the table. I cover it with a notebook.

My mind goes back to Basil. The pangs of guilt for doing my job have tripled since our kiss on the beach days ago. I wish I could rewind to yesterday, to us celebrating our victory in every room of the villa, all night and this morning. Our other reward for second place, the black box with a red bow, is sitting on the kitchen countertop, but we didn't get a chance to open it before her meeting started.

Recalling the way Basil looks at me and how my heart swells when she does, I know we care about each other. Being involved with someone and having this level of distrust is not sitting right with me. Never has.

Juliette returns and unmutes herself. "My apologies." She shakes her head and sighs. "An employee is claiming a work-related injury despite a video on social media possibly proving otherwise. Looks like I'll be needing a worker's compensation investigation as well. We can discuss details when you return to Seattle."

People be peopling. I nod.

Juliette opens her mouth to say something. "Let's move on—"

"Caroline?" My name is yelled.

Basil. With wide eyes, I slam the End button and turn.

My shoulders relax. Thankfully, I locked the bedroom door. I clear my throat and respond.

"Be out in a minute."

"I got the deal! Let's celebrate tonight."

I inhale and release the air in my lungs to regain composure. From the other room, I can hear Basil's bag hitting the entryway bench. She reminds me our next itinerary event starts in less than ten minutes, which was the last thing on my mind. She sounds like she's in a good mood, and I don't want to change that; meanwhile, my heart and mind are at war.

Do I drop the case and a long-standing client? Is quitting Basil even an option at this point? How will Juliette respond to my breaking our agreement? At least she won't be able to use the trip to Sapphire Isle against me. I'll pay her back as soon as I land in Seattle, but she might take critical jabs at my reputation or worse.

I stand and grab the back of my neck. I better change at least one article of clothing while I think of next steps. I leisurely walk toward my folded stack of T-shirts in the closet and pull the middle one from the pile. If I do quit, when do I tell Basil the truth about the case? Or should I not confess anything at all?

I change into my v-neck and refold the two on top deep in thought. No. I need to tell her. Fear of the end of us plagues my heart, but the thought of continuing another day lying to her is unbearable. It's bad enough that her mother is breaking her trust. With two strides, I'm at the nightstand. Phone. Wallet. Sunscreen. Check. I know, deep down, Basil should learn the truth and be the one to make the decision if she still wants me in her life. Whatever I do, I need to choose before leaving this island.

Easier said than done. I'm breaking all the rules I put in place years ago, the ones to protect me from getting my heart broken, which now feels inevitable.

Mind still racing, I peer into the standing mirror and adjust my hair. I tilt my head as I move the strands of coils where I want them. There's no use in comparing this situation to my past. Grace *knew* I was a private investigator before we met and actively sought to manipulate me in favor of her divorce asset case. She never loved me. I recall the coldness in her eyes when she didn't get the results she wanted and how useless she said I was. Everything was all a lie for her. My feelings for Basil are not. I put my hand on the doorknob to leave, but pause and take a breath.

I've already risked my career once for a chance at love. Is it worth doing again?

CHAPTER 22

CAROLINE

BASIL TUGS my hand to speed up our walk down the resort hallway toward the workshop. Apparently, she's quite excited about Queer Finances 101.

When we pass the open double doors for the event, I yank around and point to redirect us. "We missed the entrance."

"I know," she says with that cunning smile that tells me she's up to no good. "We're not going inside."

We turn the corner and pace down the hallway. The lights seem to dim the further go; this is a path I haven't traveled before. "Where are you taking me?"

She doesn't answer. We continue until the sounds of the chatter becomes faint, almost nonexistent. The only sounds remaining are my increasing heartbeat and the off-and-on rumbling thunder from the stormy weather. She halts and points. "Here."

I silently assess the tiny screen on the side and red curtain and crinkle my brows together in confusion. "A photo booth?" I can't remember the last time I was inside one.

"The Blakemans gave me a quick tour. Apparently, people rarely ever go down here since there's nothing but this photo booth, which they plan to get rid of next month. This hallway is not included on the patron tour; I just happened to inquire about renovations." She chuckles and slides the fabric open. "Don't get me wrong, I love to talk about money just as much as the next person, but I'm wearing my favorite sundress, so I thought we could take pictures."

I'm not buying it. "For an hour?" I give her a look. "That's a lot of photos."

She nods, a glint of seduction in her eyes. She knows I'm picking up on her. "I can think of some creative poses to pass the time. Let's call this a continuation of our celebration." That devilishly cute dimpled grin returns. "This is better than walking back to the villa. It's pouring outside." She points an index finger toward the ceiling.

We pause for a moment and listen. Pitter-patter drops of rain pound against the rooftop. It seems like the rain is coming down sideways. I hear storms don't last long on the island but can be intense when they arrive. Maybe she has a point.

I glance around. At least there's no one else here—they're probably in the workshop, which, from the sounds of clapping, isn't that far away. I don't know if being alone with Basil is good or bad at this point, given she's still my target and we can't seem to keep our hands off each other. I shake my head because *this* keeps happening. Giving into my temptation, I enter first and sit on the black cushion. There's barely room for two. What a time to have long legs and a fierce desire to push Basil's face between them. *Pictures only, then destroy the photo-booth strip,* I tell myself—the evidence of the forbidden relationship between us.

She sits down next to me and drops her tote bag by her legs onto the floor. When she leans across to close the curtain, I inhale the scents of mandarin and jasmine from her perfume, and I wonder if I'll miss it when I'm back in Seattle.

Because that's the reality of the situation. We're not in a real relationship. For her, I'm probably a temporary fix from being left at the altar. My jaw tightens at the thought, and I stare at the wall.

"What's going on?" Basil gently brushes my shoulder with hers and finds my eyes "You've been acting strange since we left the villa."

I hesitate, fighting the urge to say what's on my mind. The words spill anyway. "We don't have much time left on the island together." I clamp my eyes shut, and the painful truth comes out. "Basil, I know what this is. I'm just a distraction from the pain. A rebound, but I can't—" I pause, unsure how to explain. Keep falling—to the point where I'm madly, deeply in love with my target, whose mother I'm working for?

"I don't believe that's how I feel." She pushes her loose curls to one side and caresses my fingers. "I know it looks that way, but for me it's—I don't know. Complicated? I feel things that I probably shouldn't be feeling right now. Not in the amount of time we've spent together."

I expel a breath. "You know that I don't like to start things I can't finish. I mean that."

Silence.

She stands and turns. Somehow, she manages to straddle me in this tiny photo booth and wrap her arms around my neck, prompting me to hold her waist. The way her eyes soften when we're this close makes my stomach flip and flop. I love the way she looks at me.

"Yes, I admit this was all unexpected." Her voice is full of tenderness. She readjusts her position so we're both more comfortable. "But I'm learning to not always question synchronicities." Her lips brush mine, and I can't help but melt into the kiss. "I wish you could see what I see." She huffs a breath and whispers, "I think I'm falling in love with you."

There's raw emotion in her eyes that tells me she's being sincere. We stare into each other's souls for a beat. Can she see how much I care for her? How conflicted my brain gets when she touches me? Or how royally screwed I am?

"Basil. I—"

Lips on my neck cut me off. A satisfying moan escapes my mouth as she trails tiny kisses to my earlobe. All thoughts of the impossibilities between us vanish. My grip around her waist tightens. I never want to let her go.

"Let's just enjoy the time we have and then figure out the rest later." She kisses me gently on the lips. "Besides, I didn't bring you here only for pictures. Close your eyes."

I oblige and wonder what she's up to when I sense her body weight shift and hear her rustling in her bag.

"Is this okay?"

My eyelids flutter open. A black silk blindfold?

"Do you trust me?" she asks, a smirk painting her lips.

"Yes." I lean forward so she has room to tie the fabric around my head.

Stillness stretches between us. The only sounds I hear are the taps of the rain outside and our heartbeats. Gentle strokes of her fingers up and down my cheek relax every fiber in my body. No matter what happens next, I trust Basil.

My flurry of anticipation breaks when something soft—featherlike—caresses my clavicle. The sensitive skin goose-bumps, and a shiver travels up my spine.

She leans in and whispers. "I figured out what 'SM' means. Care to know?"

I lick my lips. She opened the black box with the red bow without me. I can't help the mischievous grin forming. I probe my mind for the most salacious answers, but say none of them. "What?"

"*Sapphic Mischief.*" She laughs. "There was a lot more than a feather and a blindfold inside that box. So many things that I have yet to try."

A light sensation, so careful it barely touches my skin, travels the borders of my tank top, tickling the valley of my breasts and then traveling down my arms.

"I can't stop thinking about that night," she confesses.

She doesn't have to explain which one. It's etched in my mind too. A kaleidoscope of images of my hand around her neck while I voraciously kissed her against the hotel door circles my mind. I remember the feeling of her wetness through her clothes when my leg pressed between her thighs. I'll never forget the way she begged to taste me or how badly I wanted her that same instant. And certainly not how hard I came with just a few flicks of her tongue.

I return to the present. We're both winning at this tantalizing game of sensory deprivation. My breathing shallows and my other senses enhance with each featherlight stroke.

I empty the air in my lungs when the tip of her tongue teases the spot on my neck that she knows gets me every time.

The feather seems out of the picture now. My hand lifts from her waist, and the next thing I feel is her warm breath and wetness as she puts my finger in her mouth. The vibration from her delicious moan when she wets it sends jolts of desire from my fingertip to my already throbbing pussy lips.

The same hand moves down between our bodies, underneath her sundress, and the pulsing between my thighs skyrockets when I discover she's not wearing panties. She doesn't have to show me what to do next.

Our mouths fuse together. I spread my legs wider, granting me more access by opening her further as well. She gasps when I ease a finger into her, then another, coating them with her wetness.

She moans how good it feels. I thrust harder, yet slowly

and with determination. I wish I could see her face, the little flush in her cheeks when she's close.

"Caroline," she pants my name, triggering my other hand to grip her hips and rock her forward.

"Fuck," I growl while I'm tugging her into my measured, forceful thrusts. "I can smell how much you want me." She's soaked. We both are, and we're only getting started.

"I'm going to come all over your fingers, aren't I?"

She's taunting me to go faster. I can hear it in her voice. We both know she's well aware of the answer.

Instead of giving her what she wants right away, I press my thumb on her swollen clit and switch my rhythm to slow and steady circles. This cramped position is making my already burning forearms ache with more pain, but I'm not stopping.

Just as I increase my speed, her hand slides past the elastic of my pants and underneath my boy shorts. My legs drift as wide as hers on top let me, to offer more space for her hand. She wastes no time gliding a finger into me, reminding me of her impatience.

My eyes roll at how good she feels inside me. We work simultaneously, rowing at a steady pace. When I sense her lips close to mine, I trap her moans with my mouth, and our tongues explore.

I curl my fingers against the sponge inside. Her moans turn to high-pitched whimpers, and her muscles clamp down on my fingers as I continue. With a few more flicks of my thumb, her whole body tenses. Her teeth sink into my shoulder to suppress her scream of pleasure as her juices flood into my palm. Her final thrusts against my walls combined with the sensation of her climax launch me over the edge. I dig my fingers into her hips and cry out, any self-consciousness getting thrown out the window.

We continue kissing while I ride the tremors flowing

through my body. Her legs are hot against mine. I know they're tired like mine. We extract our fingers and she rests her head on my shoulder prompting me to wrap my arms around her waist. I hold her limp body and appreciate all the little noises she's making that tells me she's satisfied. Her exhausted giggle makes me smile.

After a couple of minutes of listening to her breathing, my heart rate returns to normal. The fabric covering my eyes gets removed. I blink to gather my bearings, and when my vision comes into focus, Basil's hooded eyes are all I see. Beads of sweat on her forehead tell me she's deliciously spent.

She looks me in the eyes. "I don't have all of the answers, but I know I don't want this to end." She places a tender kiss on the lips, then my nose and back to my mouth. "That's how I feel."

I think for a moment. Everything I told myself I wouldn't do with my target, I did. My lips did. My tongue did. My heart did. Thoughts of the case long gone, I kiss her again and offer a reassuring smile. "It won't."

She climbs off my lap and returns to sitting next to me. We settle on taking pictures even in our sweaty condition. I don't think we've giggled this much in one day before. During the last photo, using a finger, I tilt her chin toward me and brush our lips together like it's the last kiss we'll ever have.

We part, and she lifts from my lap and stands. She grabs the strip of photos and holds them up. "You're adorable and photogenic. I think we make a cute couple."

I grin at our poses and take the strip of photos and slide it into my pocket. "I'll keep it safe from the rain."

"I feel like I should make a 'Slippery When Wet' joke." We laugh as she adjusts her dress, flattening the front to get rid of the evidence of the naughty things we just did. All I know is I'll never look at a photo booth the same again.

My phone vibrates in my pocket. Juliette, I assume. The reminder that I should be staying away from Basil—yet here we were. Checking the notification sooner than later might be a good idea now that I'm in the hot seat for challenging Juliette and then hanging up on her. I think of an excuse and hope Basil doesn't question. "It might be better if you walk out first in case someone heard us."

"Okay, I'll meet you up front." She pecks my lips. "Let's continue this back at the villa."

Once Basil's gone, I remove my phone from my pocket and check the notification.

JULIETTE
I need an update.

CAROLINE
I will call this evening.

Today. In two hours.

I grip my phone in frustration. There's no more war inside my heart. I know what I want now: Basil. Without further contemplation, I fire off another message.

It will be our last meeting. I quit.

CHAPTER 23

BASIL

I WAKE up to the island rays peeking through the sheer curtains and the sounds of the ocean colliding into the deck. I reach for Caroline on her side of the bed, but feel nothing but the coolness of empty sheets. She must have gone for a run. Sitting up, I glance at the pile of pillows in the corner, the ones used for the pillow wall I put up what feels like years ago. Now, I appreciate being engulfed in Caroline's warmth during mornings and nights. With no more scheduled events to attend, we have the remaining days on the island all to ourselves. Maybe with enough kisses for encouragement, we can spend them in bed. Then again, the romantic scavenger hunt Lynn told me was happening today seems like an event Caroline would enjoy.

My phone dings, and without looking, I grab it from the nightstand to read the notification. The airline's reminder for check-in is looming. Days on Sapphire Isle have gone somehow quickly and slowly at the same time. The thought of returning to Seattle rejuvenated yet alone isn't as appealing or empowering as I had hoped. Not that I believe in magic spells, but a part of me wished I could return home

—Riley and Hazel's place for now—feeling like my old self. Deep down, I know that's impossible after the type of breakup I've had, but more so since meeting Caroline.

Two days have passed since we talked inside the photo booth. I don't agree that she's a rebound, but I do believe I've found it quite easy to circumvent my emotions. To be fair, I've been avoiding most parts of my life—Mother, being left at the altar, and countless work emails. Continuing this behavior forever won't end well. One thing I've learned is if I ever go on a honeymoon again, I'm not bringing *anything* relating to the office. Even though I succeeded at making the wine deal with the Blakemans, interacting with Lynn and Mae doesn't feel like work. Observing how they approach business and marriage happily as a team makes me wonder if that's something I could obtain one day. Certainly not underneath my mother's shadow.

A smile tugs at my lips picturing Caroline and myself on the championship podium, silver medals wrapped around our necks. We make a great team.

When I return my phone to the nightstand, I discover a note.

Went for a run. Will bring breakfast. XO —Caroline

Rereading her scribbled words on the mini notepad, I realize, it's the little things about her that I love—how she makes me laugh without trying and the sense of ease I feel in her presence, in her arms. How the weight of her gaze makes my body tingle with salacious desire. I've rarely experienced letting someone into my heart in such a short time, something I vowed to *never* do again, but here I am. I don't need a therapist to tell me my parents projected their failed marriage onto their children or that I'm naturally suspicious of others. But someone *could* help explain the way my heart sings for Caroline.

I slip into a robe and walk to the sliding door, but I only stand in front of it, peering out at the endless ocean. For the next ten minutes, I ponder how I'm going to prove to Caroline how much I still want her in my life when we arrive back in Seattle. What do people do? Movies, museums, cooking together—I have no idea how modern-day dating fits in my busy schedule. Then again, spending quality time together with people I care about wasn't a priority for me in the past, which I will change moving forward. Looking back on how I showed up in my last relationship, there's so much I'd change.

Yes, Riley was right. I know time heals wounds, allowing people to process, forgive, and trust, but being with Caroline is so...*effortless*. Or am I naive to think jumping from one relationship to the next—no matter how strong my feelings are—is a wise decision?

There's a knock on the front door. I shake my head with a smile, recalling opening the door earlier this week. Caroline's hands were full with enough pastries to feed a small village, and she'd almost spilled a latte when handing me my order. That could've happened in Seattle if I hadn't ghosted her. The gesture was kind, and I didn't *want* to leave, but I had no choice. Have I ever made my own decisions about what I want?

On the second knock, I force the thoughts away and pace to the foyer, yelling, "Coming, Caroline!"

There's a third knock, and my smile widens. I'm giddy like a teenager. I swing the door open. The blood drains from my face.

"*Mother!?*"

CHAPTER 24

CAROLINE

AFTER SPRINTING MY FINAL STRETCH, I rest my hands on top of my head and steady my breathing from slugging each footstep through the sand. I'm getting better at running on the beach—this is resistance training with a gorgeous view. The task has proved more difficult than it looked, but being exposed to the cool morning air and nature does more for my mind and heart than a treadmill any day.

I pass the resort's front desk and pause to retrieve my phone vibrating in my shorts pocket. It's a text message from the café notifying me that my order is ready. I've learned my lesson on impulse ordering. Only four items this time.

"Speaking of Mrs. Jones." I hear someone behind me and turn. Sunny hangs up her desk phone and taps her keyboard a few times. She looks at me with a kind smile. "Your arranged transportation will be here shortly."

I tilt my head, a grin painted across my lips. "What's my wife up to now?" Our romantic beach lunch date was a nice surprise. Minus the jellyfish interruption.

Sunny cracks a laugh, like I'm the funniest person in the world, but I don't get the joke. "I'm going to miss you two when you leave. Let me know if you need any further assistance with your departure."

Okay... I guess I'll ask Basil when I get back to the villa. "Sure. Thanks, Sunny." I turn to walk away.

"How do you do it so well?"

I halt and yank my attention to her. "What do you mean?"

She chews her bottom lip. "Marriage. You and Mrs. Jones appear...unapologetically in love. More than most that stay on this island." She peers at the wall, a slight blush in her cheeks, then she pulls her hair to one side. "Asking for a friend."

I recall the conversation with Lynn and Akari at The Tiki Taco. "A friend, huh?"

"It's complicated." She chuckles, rolling her eyes. "You'd think I'd be a relationship expert working at a place like this. It seems like an impossible task."

I chuckle. "Don't I know it."

When her gaze casts downward, I can tell she's thinking about someone. I scramble for something to say.

"Be honest and tell them how you feel. We can't expect someone to be fully honest when we aren't radically honest with ourselves first."

She faces me, and a small smile tugs at her lips. "I'll give it a try. Thanks."

I flash her a friendly wink. "Good luck."

After waving goodbye, I go to pick up the food and continue on my journey to see my favorite dimpled grin. By the time I leave the café, I know I'm going to take my own advice. The case is over. There's nothing left to do but tell Basil the truth and spend the rest of our time on this island together.

I enter the villa and peer toward the center of the room. The wind knocks out of me. Juliette is sitting on the couch, one leg crossed over the other. Her eyes are as pitch black as her suit, and the cunning smile tugging at her lips points right at me. Papers and pictures lie scattered on the coffee table. My jaw drops, as does the small container of food in my hand. Sounds of cracking plastic hit the air. The next thing I see is Basil standing by the window, facing me with bloodshot eyes, evidence of stale tears. *No.*

I scramble to place the items on the entryway bench. "Let me explain. Please Basil."

Arms folded over her chest, she screams, "Explain *what*? That your"—she uses her hands as air quotes—"'consulting' business means you're a fucking private investigator? This has all been a game to you!" Her brows pinch together. "Clearly, I can't trust *anyone* in my family except Hazel." Her glare bounces from her mother to me. "But you, Caroline—" Her voice cracks with emotion. "You completely blindsided me."

I take two steps forward, but I halt, my feet stuck in quicksand of my guilt. "I'm so sorry." I hold an open palm out. "Please—okay, yes. I know how bad this looks. It started off as a job, but then—"

"But then it turned out you're a hell of an actress?" She huffs. "I really ought to hire you. I've never had an employee so committed to their 'job.' None of this was real for you."

Mouth agape, I nod. "Yes, it's real." I attempt to explain from the beginning, tripping over my words like a bumbling idiot, then I pause to start again. "I didn't know that this would happen when we met at the hotel."

"You didn't know what?"

"That you would turn out to be my target and that I'd fall—"

"Don't." She points to her heart, then mine with a wobbly chin "This doesn't matter, because you mean *nothing* to me." Our memories together and the hurt in her eyes tell me otherwise. "You never did."

No. No. No. I shake my head frantically. "That can't be true...please don't say that." Despite the lump in my throat, I continue, "I love you, Basil."

The room freezes. This is not how I envisioned the first time telling Basil my true feelings. Tears stream down her cheeks, shattering my heart into a million pieces.

Silence.

We stare at each other for what feels like eternity, until she wipes her tears carefully with a tissue. I open my mouth to speak, but no words come out, only a heavy breath filled with shame, hurt, and loss.

"Get out." Her icy tone sends a jarring chill down my spine. She points to the door, then diverts her gaze out the window, her eyes cold enough to freeze the glass. "Just leave." Her words are barely audible, but the message is clear. We're over.

"Basil—"

"Ms. King," Juliette interrupts. She stands and approaches me with her arm stretched out. A flash of pain etches her face, as if she's realizing the magnitude of the situation as well as the consequence of her arrival. She purses her lips. "You don't get the luxury of quitting for *love*. You're fired."

I look down at the piece of paper shoved in front of me. A ticket for an early flight back to Seattle. The warmth and fullness that canvassed my heart minutes ago is gone, replaced with a persistent, hollow ache. "I—"

"Your flight leaves today. I'd hate for you to miss it." She returns to her seat and takes a sip of her water. "I'm not paying for another one."

Somehow, I blink back my tears and dismiss Juliette's last words, then direct my attention to the shellshocked woman in front of me.

"Basil, I'm so sorry. It wasn't supposed to be like this. *Please* hear me out," I beg through the stinging sensation at the corner of my eyes. "I love you," I whisper. When I'm met with more silence, a sickness churns my stomach. The fight in my heart is depleted, leaving me with complete emptiness.

With slumped shoulders, I turn, grab my bag, and leave the villa—but not the memories—my feet feeling ten times heavier than they did during my beach run earlier this morning. I meet Basil's misty eyes once more before the wooden door slams in my face. The forceful thud echoes through my veins, and I hear Basil's heavy sobs unleash from the other side. She's in so much pain, and I'm not there to hold her.

I caused her so much pain.

Hopeless, I wrap my arms around my waist and lean my back onto the door, my eyes clamped shut. Each weep from Basil's mouth hits like a violent strike against the barricade holding back my tears. Unable to stop thoughts of the past from flooding in, finally I break too.

I did this to myself. This is why I don't do love—everyone leaves me in the end. And it's my fault.

I wipe my wet face with the back of my hand and walk away, passing the idling car in front of the villa entrance. I head toward the bar. Basil would have never chosen me, anyway.

CHAPTER 25

BASIL

"Are you happy now?" I address my mother when she joins me an hour later on the deck. We're the same regarding needing space when we're upset, but this time, too much damage has been done. She left me alone barely long enough for me to put on a sundress and start rage-packing—shoving fistfuls of clothes into my luggage bag. I never finished. I had to step away. Everything I touched reminded me of Caroline. I need a decade, not an hour. "Clearly, I'm the only person in this family that isn't allowed to be."

Behind me, Juliette doesn't respond. I feel a hand on my elbow, which I brush off immediately. "No," I growl. "You've outdone yourself this time. A private investigator?" I shake my head.

There are so many questions swirling inside my mind, but the most painful one slips out. "Did you pay her to pretend to fall in love—" The sob stuck in my throat prevents me from finishing the sentence. I don't think I can handle that answer on top of everything else that's happened.

"No." Juliette stands beside me, arms crossed over her chest, her lips pressed into a thin line. We even pout the same. "Makes sense why she tried to quit the case. Unfortunately, that little declaration of love caught both of us by surprise. "

And I loved Caroline too, but how do I know what was real and what wasn't when she was lying to me? My gaze points over the water, and I change the subject back and demand more answers. "Is this the first time you've hired someone to follow me?" I can't believe I'm asking this question to my own *parent*.

"It's the one and only time."

"I don't believe you," I blurt out. How can I?

"It's true. I hired Ms. King to watch you from a distance. Clearly, that didn't happen."

I huff, then tighten my fingers around the rails until my knuckles turn white. No breathing exercise could calm me down at this moment. I try anyway. After a few deep breaths, I trace the outlines of the tan and gray stones resting underneath the clear water while the sounds of gentle waves lap the shore. It helps a little, but the ache from heartbreak and betrayal continues to slowly expand in my chest.

"Why?" I ask. The word comes out in a hollow whisper. I face her, needing to look into her eyes. "Seeing your daughter being left at the altar and getting her heart destroyed wasn't enough for you?"

Our gazes hold, silence stretching between us. She seems surprised at my words—or maybe it's my sharp tone, which she hasn't heard for longer than three minutes without my apologizing.

She's doing her typical thing, always taking her damn time to respond. Unlike her, I've never had enough patience to hide my emotions well. I glare at her, wishing the storm raging in me could spill out and crash all over her calm, perfect head.

"I want the truth for once," I demand.

She drops her arms to her sides and exhales. "I wanted to give you space, but I also needed to know nothing would interfere with the wine deal that we've been working incredibly hard to obtain—that *you've* been working hard to obtain. Hiring Ms. King was the best solution I could think of with the limited time I had."

"I knew the real reason involved work. It always does with you."

"Do not villainize me. I'm your mother. I just want you to have the best life. I think you and Olivia—"

"Don't," I snap. "Don't you *dare* say that name right now."

Silence.

I can sense more angry tears coming on, but I look away to compose myself. I've cried enough in front of people today. This is the first time I've ever stood up to Juliette, but I don't think I can continue living underneath her microscope. It's too controlling. Being free from her for almost two weeks has changed how I view my autonomy, and as much as I don't want to admit it, being with Caroline has also changed me.

I speak my thoughts out loud against my better inclinations, like an idiot. "The sad truth is, I had more feelings for the woman who walked out that front door after two weeks than I had with a woman I was with for over seven years. What's wrong with me?"

"Sweetheart." A gentle hand lands on my shoulder. Juliette's voice turns into that manipulative, motherly tone I know all too well. "An island affair is just that. It's intense and burns hot, then it's over. Time to go back to reality." When I pull away again, she adds, "You have a promotion waiting for you when we get back. That's what you want, isn't it? You deserve it. Look alive. Let's go home."

I felt alive with Caroline. I see right through my mother this time and dismiss her last words. "It wasn't just a fling." I blink twice, not caring that I sound like a lovesick teenager. Now over this conversation, I walk away and pause at the sliding door before opening it. "Not for me. I swear, I loved Caro—"

"Love is not enough!" Her heel slamming into the deck floor freezes my hand gripping the handle. "It's foolish to think so." Her voice goes soft. "Like I did. I'm trying to protect you."

When I see her reflection through the glass, I'm met with a vulnerability looming over her that I hadn't noticed before. The way the corners of her eyes crinkle with concern tells me she's running out of cards to play.

I face her. "You know what hurts the most?" I search my brain to string together the right sentences in a language she'll hopefully understand. The only words remaining are the ones in my heart. "You betrayed my trust in the most unimaginable way. Not only as my mother, but as my colleague. How could you expect me to speak to you, let alone still want to work for you after this?" I scoff. "You didn't call to check on me, only your precious legacy. You haven't once asked me what I want or even apologized for hurting me."

"Give me a chance and I will apologize."

"Okay." I pause, waiting for her to say the magic words, as if saying "sorry" will open a portal for us to travel back in time.

Seconds go by, and nothing. This time, I'm not waiting for her to speak. It's futile anyway. "You might as well leave. I'm not flying back home with you, Juliette."

"I'll be downstairs when you change your mind."

"I won't."

Thankfully, she leaves without fighting for the last word. After slamming the front door for the second time today, I crawl into bed, feeling more lost than I have in years. I know she was attempting to help in her own twisted way, but I'm sick and tired of her projecting her failed marriage onto our family.

Then again, I know she's not entirely wrong. Love isn't enough...but what is?

I've invested so much of myself into a wine business that I don't even know if I truly want it in my life now.

Then again, maybe Mother is right: Maybe if I go back to reality, these feelings will fade. After all, what about Lynn and Mae? And I can't leave my family business and all the opportunities waiting for me back in Seattle. Plus, this promotion is everything I've been working toward, and now it's mine.

A part of me despises the thought of working for my mother, but I know long-term, the business will be there. Love may not.

I'll lie here a while longer before joining my mother downstairs to fly back to Seattle. I squeeze the pillow, and Caroline's scent engulfs my entire being. I hate that I miss her already. But I do.

CHAPTER 26

CAROLINE

THE TIKI TACO isn't crowded this morning. There's no Akari, either. As much as I appreciate her exuberance, I need alone time with a cold beer to wash down the taste of failure from losing Basil and taking a knock to my career in the process.

As a distraction from my thoughts, I'm sitting at the bar watching a couple building a sand castle on the beach. They go from bickering to exchanging high-fives in ten minutes. It reminds me of when I desperately searched for the whistle during Round One of the Sapphic Olympics, determined to prove Basil wrong, and then of us celebrating her tying the Gladiator Strike record.

None of that matters anymore. Maybe coming to Sapphire Isle wasn't the change in scenery I needed. Moving to a new city will be. It's what always works at the end of the day. I can already hear Kaydence's disappointment-laced tone. She'll probably tell me I'll be leaving Seattle for the wrong reasons—running to escape my problems—and she'll be right.

A familiar laugh interrupts my train of thought. I peek

over my shoulder and sure enough, Lynn's coming my way, wearing a tank top and shorts, no scarf around her neck.

With a grin as bright as the sun, she looks at me, then around the bar, and asks the obvious question. "No partner in crime today? Mine got an early start at the office."

"Not today…" I trail off, unable to meet her eyes when she sits on the barstool next to me. This time, I'm somewhat relieved by her presence. "Maybe not *ever*."

"Uh oh. That's not good. Did you two get into a nasty argument?"

That, and I'm an idiot. I exhale and unfold my hands, then rest the bottle opening on my bottom lip before tipping it for a swig. "Yeah, you could say that."

My eyes remain fixed on the beer label. I can sense the wheels churning upstairs as she assesses me, her weighted gaze strengthening with each second. Without another word, she looks away and orders a drink.

During our silence, the bartender sets a cold beer on the bartop in front of Lynn. She shifts her body toward me. "You know, it's not uncommon to have a heated argument during your honeymoon. There can be a lot of pent-up residual emotions from the wedding chaos." She chuckles. "Mae and I didn't talk to each other for half a day after a quarrel over me not acting romantic enough *during* a scuba diving excursion."

The image of Lynn alone in a wetsuit elicits a tiny laugh from me. Appreciating her effort to cheer me up and out of genuine curiosity, I ask, "What brought you two back together?"

"A good dose of courage and even better timing. We received some of the finished pictures from the wedding. I got them laminated, then jumped into a tank filled with sharks and held them up for the world to see."

Her tone warms as she smiles. "All our memories served as a reminder of how far we had come and promised a future worth taking more pictures of. Mae was so gorgeous in her wedding dress. I was a mess when I first saw her. The photographer said she'd never see anyone cry as much as I did. What I'm saying is, it doesn't mean the end of your relationship. It's just a good excuse for more kissing and making up later."

Unfortunately, time isn't on my side. I pull my bottom lip between my teeth in thought. "I don't know if there's anything that could save us. Plus, we're taking separate flights back to Seattle. I screwed up pretty badly." That's an understatement.

"Mae and I have had our struggles too." Lynn takes a long pull from her beer. "Remember me talking about exes?"

I nod.

"Believe it or not, years ago, I swore I'd never get married."

That grabs my attention. I tilt my head in disbelief. "*You?* I don't believe it," I say. "And you're still going strong thirty-plus years later. Who would've thought?"

"Certainly not this freedom-seeking bird." She laughs. "Mae and I had been dating for a few years, and she wanted to get married, but I wasn't ready. How could I've been? Her family seemed to hate me before they met me because I'm a woman. They weren't exactly fond that I didn't share their culture either. They never admitted the second part out loud, but I could feel it."

"What happened?"

Lynn pauses until a rowdy group of people passes. "One day, I gave Mae an ultimatum: no marriage or we were done, which went about as well as one could imagine. For as long as I've known her, she has always danced to the beat of her own drum. Her parents knew not to push her. I wish I had known. If you think Mae is prickly now, you should've seen her twenty years ago. Even her compliments sounded like commands. Anyway, everything became this massive cluster-fuck fight ending with me pouring out my real reason for not committing—fear."

Lynn continues, "She asked me if I loved her enough to work it out. I said no, because no matter how much we loved each other, I was terrified she'd end up listening to her parents and leave me anyway. Her side of the closet was empty before I could blink. Years later, we ran into each other at the Clean Energy Expo. She was married to someone who was everything I wasn't. But we worked out in the end."

Sounds of crushing ice inside a blender catch my attention. The scent of orange juice and champagne teases my nose when the person next to me retrieves their drink. I didn't know frozen mimosas existed. My focus shifts back to Lynn, who hadn't stopped talking.

"The hardest part wasn't forgiving myself." Her face turns serious. "It was holding her again and realizing the time we'd lost. That was five years of kisses, arguments, and love I won't get back. My advice? Give Basil some time, but don't wait years like I did. If you love her, go get her. If she doesn't love you back, then at least you won't have to wonder."

I nod. I know that feeling all too well. The more I think about how to get Basil back, the more discouraged I get. None of my scenarios end with an epic love story like Lynn and Mae's.

"Wait. How did you two get back together?" I ask. "Let me guess: a good dose of courage and even better timing."

"And luck." She pushes her sunglasses over her eyes and makes a contemplative sound. "I heard the dumb bloke ran off with *her* secretary. I happened to be in the job market and got an interview." She chuckles, and that bright smile is back. "I didn't get the position, but I got the girl."

We fist bump. "I'm glad. You two seem great together." I

mean every word. I exhale a breath. "Thank you. That gives me hope."

She does the same, an indication that storytime is over. Back to reality. "When you two are all made up, we'll plan something fun. I like to think we've become friends."

She swings an arm around my shoulders and gives me a reassuring hug. If only she knew the truth, the one that's not mine to tell. I know how much Basil's relationship with the Blakemans means to her, and I've already hurt her enough. The thought of never seeing Lynn or Mae again stings more than I care to admit.

I check the departure time on my ticket. "My flight leaves in two hours. I'm sorry, but I have to go." I lift my beer in the air. "I wish I could stay and enjoy the view with you."

Lynn taps her bottle against mine, and we take a final drink. After standing, she pats my back. "Come on. Let's go grab the hog and I'll take you to catch your plane. He always makes me feel better."

"Would it be okay if I took a quick shower at your place?" I'd rather not sit on a plane in my workout clothes.

"Of course. You're welcome anytime."

We begin our descent to the shore. Five minutes of silence later, Lynn shoves her hands in her pockets. "You know, me and Quilliam are really going to miss you. You're a good person to be around. Promise me you'll visit?"

I do my best to muster a smile through the sadness. I don't know if she'll feel the same way if she learns about Basil and me. Or if I'll visit alone. Nonetheless, it's a promise I plan to keep. "I will, friend."

CHAPTER 27

BASIL

THE LAST SIX months have been hectic and exhausting, to say the least, but in a good way. It's the dark, gloomy winter sky that makes me miss the perfect island weather. Seated in my office chair, I peer out the window. This afternoon, downtown is lacking its usual vibrancy. Being from Seattle, the frigid winds never bothered me much up until recently. I had always thought the city was beautiful even during the cold and wet days, but the view isn't doing it for me right now.

My stomach growls, reminding me that I need food for survival. I have a meeting with the board of directors starting in less than thirty minutes, and I missed the window to have Jenn pick me up food. She's a great personal assistant, but she's not a miracle worker.

With a heavy exhale, I run my fingers through my hair, knowing I need to eat *something* in order to focus. I scour through my desk drawers one after another, desperately searching for anything to curb my hunger until I get home tonight—whenever that is. Reaching into the depths of the last drawer, my fingers tap a plastic wrapper. It's not empty. I yank the granola bar out and open it.

I didn't imagine this promotion would bring such joy: expired chocolate-chip granola bars and a tiny bottle of juice from the networking event two months ago. Nibbling through the stale oats, I kick off my heels and try to relax during the rare moment of silence. This is my life now. Living with people but feeling alone. Meetings stacked on top of meetings—taking over my entire day and making it difficult to complete meaningful work.

Staying with Riley and Hazel hasn't been awful, but being forced to look young love in the face every day while fighting off thoughts of Caroline is draining. A streak of anger zips up my spine, recalling the way my blood boiled when my mother showed me the manila folder, claiming for me to stop "playing house." I still can't believe Caroline betrayed me after I'd poured out my heart about being left at the altar. After all we went through, I trusted her. I fell in *love* with her. Was Caroline—assuming that's even her real name—going to tell me if my mother didn't show up.

Someone knocks on my door, interrupting my date with the muted view of the city. Grumbling underneath my breath, I slam the wrapper in the trash. I hear three more quick taps against the door, followed by two heavier ones. Riley's signature knock.

"Come in," I yell.

Riley barrels through the door and, with Jenn's help, strolls into my office carrying a baby approximately two years old in one arm and a plastic bag in the other. She plops the bag in front of me, and the smell of my favorite blackened salmon makes my mouth water.

I groan in delight. "God, I love you. Thank you." She flashes me a weak smile and sets the plastic fork on the desk. Wasting no time, I pour the Caesar dressing on top of the salad, close the lid, and shake the container to mix everything evenly. Caroline taught me that trick. She told me learned it from a friend—she probably lied about that too. When a pang of sadness hits my chest, I push the thought of her far away.

After shoveling three bites into my mouth, I don't experience the fulfillment I usually get from my favorite salad, but I'm starting to feel like myself again. Remembering that I'm not alone, I crinkle my eyebrows together at the drooling baby in Riley's arms. Who is that? She doesn't seem pleased to see me either.

I attempt to break the growing tension with a joke. "Don't tell me you and Hazel made me an aunt."

It doesn't land. She boosts the child up her hip. "This is my nephew, Ollie. My brother is in town from Ohio." She tilts her head and gives me a look that tells me I'm in trouble. "We had an entire discussion on Monday about you meeting us for lunch." Her brows scrunch together at my confusion. "Meet at the restaurant at 11 a.m. Thursday…three hours ago?

My eyes go wide. "Shit—I mean shoot."

"I called you six times."

I reach for my phone, wondering why it didn't ring, then I remember it's buried in my bag somewhere on silent mode. "I don't even know what day it is."

"*Thursday*," she repeats.

"Right. Sorry." I grab the bottle of juice and twist it open, take a whiff, and recant my decision. Maybe the drink has been inside my desk longer than two months. I've lost track of time at this point. I push it to the side. "I've been discombobulated with work. Can I make it up to you?"

Directing my attention back to my laptop, I scroll through my calendar. "I have a free lunch hour next Wednesday before I fly to Maryland for a demo." I'll actually create the calendar reminder this time.

"Don't worry about me. Try eating some real food."

Luckily for me, she never stays mad for long. As if reading my mind, she flashes a grin, coos at the little one, and changes her voice to baby talk. "Ollie, wouldn't it be fun to see Auntie Basil bite the cis men's heads off because she's Miss Grumpy Pants when she's hungry?" The baby giggles and paws at her scrunched face. "I'd love that sight too."

"I do eat real food."

"Then want to explain what that is?"

I follow her gaze to my trash can full of empty wrappers.

"I'm worried about you." She slowly lowers into the chair across from me, concern written on her face. "Something is definitely up if you've resorted to eating this amount of processed carbs. You've also been pretty distracted lately. Do you remember the movie from last night?"

I think for a second. Honestly, not really. "I was present... but wasn't paying much attention."

My mind has been preoccupied with what everyone else wants. To be fair, it's difficult to focus on anything at home with Riley and Hazel sucking face every ten minutes. Not to mention their frequent date nights, where they bring a whole new meaning to the words "Sleepless in Seattle."

Still, Riley has a point. I sigh in defeat and push my bitterness at my third-wheel status away. I lean back in my chair and cross one leg over the other. "Is this what I have to look forward to for the rest of my life?"

"Depends on if you want to be a clone of your mother, who makes workaholism look like an impressive skill, *or* you can go back to being the badass we know and love. Basil Version 2.0."

"She's an emotional brick wall sometimes, but she's just trying to do her best."

"A parent's best isn't always enough." She shrugs. "And that's okay. That's my conclusion, anyway. It's not fair, but they're human too."

"Basil Version 2.0 it is." Not knowing where to start, I massage my temples with my fingers. "No-judgment zone?"

"Of course." Riley confirms our code for confession time. When she sees me struggling to continue, she speaks up. "Still have your island goddess on the brain?"

A weak chuckle escapes. I nod. "And I don't know who I am anymore." I motion to my fancy office, the sleek, minimal white decorations and the skyline. "I thought this is what I wanted, but now I'm not so sure. I made amends with my mother and sacrificed my happiness, yet *again*. What's wrong with me?"

She meets my eyes. "Don't be so hard on yourself. You've been through a lot, and it's only been a handful of months since the wedding."

I nod again and sulk my gaze toward my desk. My mind travels back to the last positive image of Caroline and me together. We were cuddling in bed. For a moment, our eyes held, and I could sense she wanted to tell me something. The truth? I'll never know, because instead, she pressed her lips into my neck before compelling my hands where she wanted them. I miss her warmth.

Memories of my mother showing up, and the arguments, come crashing in. "I was so livid that I told Caroline she meant nothing to me." The hurt in her eyes remains carved in my mind. "It's the furthest thing from the truth. I know lying because my mother paid her doesn't excuse everything, but I—I fell in love with her, Riley. The real thing. I get that love's not enough though. But now I'm just empty inside."

"No, it's not. Maybe you need to start"—she points to her heart—"here first. Choosing yourself. Sometimes we need to give ourselves permission to take back our own autonomy and independence."

Before I get a chance to comment, her features light up.

She shimmies her shoulders with a smile. "I know exactly what you need."

Our go-to pick-me-up from back in college. I shake my head at her wide grin. "I don't have time for bagels, bags, and beers. I need to work."

"What you *need* is for us to grab a couple of bagels Saturday morning, shop until we drop, then wash it all down with happy-hour cold beers and good conversation. I want to hear more about this incredible sapphic island and all about the hot sex. I veto your refusal to participate."

I playfully roll my eyes. "What about all that self-help talk a minute ago?"

"I don't count."

We're sharing a laugh when Jenn knocks on the door. A reminder of my meeting starting in five minutes, which feels significantly less stressful now. Riley rises to her feet, and we exchange cheek kisses, careful of the baby.

Ollie squeezes my finger, and I can't help my smile. Riley seems like a natural with children; meanwhile, I never gave them a second thought until Caroline shared with me the funniest stories about her goddaughter. Ollie's green shirt has a happy hedgehog with a gold medal around its neck, the number one on it. My lips widen at memories of the Blake-mans, including Quilliam. I have a meeting with them in the near future that's much more exciting than the one I'm about to attend.

Before Riley leaves, I ask, curious, "Do you think you and Hazel are going to have one?" Nodding at Ollie.

She bursts with laughter, making me do the same for asking such a silly question. "Let's worry about one Jones at a time. Besides, I don't want to give your sister a heart attack. I'll see you at home."

I wave goodbye and retrieve my meeting notes from my

desk. In the hallway, I peer into my lifeless office once more, the emptiness slowly creeping back in, and shut the door.

CHAPTER 28

BASIL

THE TWO HOURS until my connecting flight to Maryland feel like years. At least the airport isn't busy so I can hear my thoughts, unlike at Seattle-Tacoma International. I'm staring at my email, sitting in the café closest to my terminal. Traveling alone for work never used to bother me, and certainly not interfere with my productivity. I'd find a cozy spot and hammer out reports while listening to podcasts, but not today.

My gaze points out the window for the third time in ten minutes. The ground is covered in snow, and air traffic control guides their light wands through the dusk sky. Minutes later, the airplane crawls toward the runway. I've lost track of how long I've been trying to finish this sentence. I tap the delete key until the *Let's catch up soon and* is gone, then I fire off the email. After closing my inbox, I click the bookmark displaying a list of available townhouses. The next phase of Basil Version 2.0.

I pause and listen to the airline making an announcement over the speakers. After verifying my terminal isn't changing,

I shove my laptop in my bag before giving into temptation to search Caroline's name on the web again.

When I lift from my chair to order food, I see someone marching toward me. I do a double take.

Victoria? My jaw tightens in exasperation.

"Don't tell me you're following me? I've had enough of that lately," I mutter when she approaches the table. Hell, I wouldn't be surprised if she was working for my mother too.

"Hi, Basil." She crosses her arms over her chest. "Do you have a minute?"

Her judgmental upper lip tells me she doesn't want to be here right now. The feeling's mutual. She smells like drama and a pending bad headache.

"Please leave. I don't have the mental capacity to deal with your misplaced vengeance right now."

She holds both palms in the air in resignation. "Trust me, I would, but—" She glances over her shoulder, then back at me. "Lauren said she'd divorce me if I didn't come over and apologize, and I love my wife more than this rivalry between us."

I huff. "Calling it a rivalry means we're on the same playing field. We're not. Life is like a game of chess, and darling, you're still struggling with the instructions."

That makes her eye twitch. She opens her mouth to say something, then closes it. Instead, she points a finger in the air. "On second thought, I'll take my chances with divorce papers." She walks away, fists balled at her sides, then halts and turns. "And you should *really* consider a refund on that personality. It's defective."

"I—" I stop myself. *Be nice, Basil.* Great. Now Caroline's words are circling my mind.

While Victoria storms off, I roll my eyes for allowing irritation to get the best of me.

Fine. Besides, I can't be involved in *every* failed relationship. At least Victoria's attempting to apologize, unlike my mother, who hasn't spoken to me about anything other than wine since leaving the island.

"Victoria, wait," I yell out. By the time she returns, I've sucked up my pride, and I motion to the seat across from me. According to most people in my life, I'm not good at this part, but I try anyway. "I'm sorry for being a jerk. It's been a long day...long months."

"I'm sorry too." She drops into the seat across from me. "We're on our way to visit my family, and I'm not looking forward to it." She rests her purse in her lap and plays with her fingers. There's an awkward silence. Now what?

I check my phone to make sure my flight hasn't been delayed. That'd be my luck, to get stuck in an airport with Victoria Miller, waiting for her to rub it in my face that Caroline's not by my side.

"Why do you hate me so much?" Victoria's words make me yank my head forward, my mouth slightly agape. "You literally ruined Ivy college opportunities for me with that billboard."

Please be serious. Rage floods through me. "You bullied my *sister* for being queer. It's not some type of common cold you just get over, Victoria. Her coming-out experience was atrocious. She got depressed..." My words trail off into nothing.

I'll never forget the day Hazel left her journal open on her bed. There were notes that she had received from other students. Some from parents. No one should ever have to go through that type of hatred—not my twin. My *heart*. We'd shared nearly everything with one another up until that point. She had been getting them for weeks, and when I'd hinted, she'd refused to tell me. Deep down, I knew she hadn't shared them out of shame. Even though there should have been *nothing* for her to hide from in the first place. Our parents weren't paying attention like I was. They were too preoccupied with their marital problems.

My gaze drifts toward a family with two young girls sharing a tablet and giggling. Although we have identical DNA, Hazel and I aren't the same in a lot of ways, but I couldn't imagine a life without her in it. Witnessing the suffering she went through and knowing the heaviness she was forced to carry—how she battled alone, no matter how reassuring my words were—was unbearable. My heart broke into a million pieces when I flipped the page in her journal and read what she wrote. She just wanted to fade away.

"Hazel almost—" I choke back tears and face Victoria. "I had to do something." I clear my throat and attempt to regain composure. "Then after all you put her through, here you are, out and proud." I huff. "I was so fucking angry when I saw you in the lobby."

She exhales. It's the first time I've seen vulnerability in her eyes. "I know, and I'm so *sorry*. I didn't know she—" She pauses. "I was sixteen and terrified of what other people would think of me—the poster child. Everything happened so fast and only got worse when I tried to explain my story. The disappointment in my parents' eyes that day haunted me for years. They changed the narrative with the school, even though I was the author of my own story. I let them."

I can tell she's struggling to hold back tears.

"Have you ever felt that way?" Through her trembling chin, she whispers, "Stuck."

My eyes withdraw from hers. She seems sincere, and although these are not the same situations, I understand the pressure of someone creating a life for you. I'd been striving to be in my mother's footsteps for so long, I didn't stop to think about what I wanted. Do I truly want to run the family business one day? Sometimes, I'm afraid of the answer.

I nod. "Yeah. I have."

"I had no clue how to voice what bisexuality was—never-mind the fact I didn't know what pansexuality was back then and it wouldn't have mattered. My parents were already so homophobic." Her gaze casts downward, then she slowly lifts her head to face me. "I liked Hazel *a lot*. I think more than she liked me, and maybe that scared me into being something I wasn't. I'm sorry; I know it's not an excuse."

"It's *not*." My tone hardens. "You have no idea the type of ridicule she went through." I sure as hell didn't come out until years later to anyone other than Hazel because of that situation.

"What do you want me to say?" She runs her fingers through her hair. Defeat is written all over her face. "I am truly sorry…" She exhales. "And I suffered too. I think having a living, breathing nonprofit literally named after your biggest mistake is payback enough. It's not exactly something I can avoid. Besides that, I couldn't simply forgive myself for hurting Hazel, someone I cared deeply about."

Creating that program seems like one of the few times I've acted on what rests in my heart, not what anyone else expects. The last time I remember being myself and not worrying about my blueprint until I was with Caroline.

Victoria continues, "I loved Lauren *light-years* before I learned to love myself. When I told her about what happened, she insisted that I forgive myself because, in her words, 'you deserve peace too.'" A weak laugh escapes her mouth. "I don't deserve Lauren. She showed me that love isn't found, because it exists in everything. We just need to realize that it's been inside of us all along. One thing is for certain: I'll never let someone else control me like society did again. Life's too short."

We drift into a long silence. She's right. Isn't ten years worth of hatred and guilt enough? Hazel only held onto her grudge for half a decade, and here I've been nurturing mine for twice that.

"Look." Victoria interrupts my train of thought. "The Blakemans talk highly of Elixir Wines, and I enjoy working with them, which means you and I have to coexist. Can we call a truce?"

I stare at her outstretched hand lingering in front of me. Hazel said she moved on. Maybe I should too. A moment passes, and I take her hand and shake it. "Truce."

"Thank you," she says, letting go. It's as if I can feel a decade of guilt melting from her shoulders. "Do you think you could help me reach out to Hazel? To apologize. Unless you think that would open up old wounds."

I nod. "Of course. I think she'd really appreciate that. The anti-bullying organization stays, of course, but I can make some phone calls to get your name removed from the website. The only way you'll be associated with it moving forward is with your consent."

"Thank you. That means a lot."

The air between us finally clears.

I stretch my stiff neck, until the tension dissipates. I guess she wasn't the only one holding onto a weight of emotions. Although I feel lighter after our talk, I'm still weary of Victoria. I don't exactly trust her but maybe one day I can.

For the next thirty minutes, we talk shop. Victoria tells me how she and Lauren got started in PR and how they connected with the Blakemans. I'm impressed to hear how she rejected her family's help and built her business from the ground up. She seems to genuinely enjoy her career, and I'm coming to respect her work ethic.

Our conversation continues as we exit and stand by the café entrance.

"I can't believe we lost to that emu woman and her fiancée," I say with a laugh. It's a shame that I let a free trip back to Sapphire Isle slip away because of my feud with Victoria.

"Right? Good for them, I guess, I heard they're having their wedding on the island now." She shakes her head. "What even *is* a hobby farmer?"

I shrug and check my phone for the time. "I'll buy you a quick drink for flipping your kayak."

"Only if you let me buy you one for calling you a pesto-mistic bitch. Although I was kind of proud of myself for that one." A nervous chuckle escapes when she meets my raised brow.

"Don't push it. We're not friends."

"*Yet.*" She smiles and points at the sports-bar sign. "Pick your poison."

Victoria and I, *friends*? Then again, I've never pictured a world where we're working together either, but here we are. Anything's possible at this point. I grab my carry-on handle and offer a grin in return. "Whatever you're having is fine. Just no mojitos."

CHAPTER 29

CAROLINE

PER THE TEXT messages from Dad, I've missed one too many family Sunday brunches. "Family" meaning "half the neighborhood crowded in front of the TV watching the latest queer reality show." In an effort to avoid having my social battery drained more than it already is from client updates, I'm here early and will leave before people start coming over. I know better than to show up late, having experienced three seasons of British baking shows, sports, and crime TV.

Sitting in the driveway, I tap my fingers on the steering wheel and admire the new paint on the exterior. Of all the houses that I lived in growing up, this bungalow is by far my favorite. The plant-green color against the white shutters adds a pop of the same vibrancy that the neighborhood already radiates. Although the previous gray color was less than five years old, the local teachers' painting crew offered a deal last summer and, based on the color selection, I have no doubt James sweet-talked Dad into that.

I reach into the front pocket of my bag to retrieve my phone, and a paper falls to the floor. When I pick it up and flip it over, my heart sinks. The photo-booth strip of Basil and me. Chewing my bottom lip, I run my thumb over the glossy finish. My favorite is the bottom picture, where I'm utterly smitten, smiling at her as she's smiling at the camera.

For a moment, I let myself get swept away in the nostalgia of us giggling while holding hands, the timer counting down and us sneaking in kisses before each flash. I'll never forget the effect of her whispered words against my skin or the feather she taunted me with inside that photo booth. Or the sounds she made when my hand slipped underneath her dress.

Even though Basil is the person I fell the hardest for, I know there's no use in trying to get her back. Her life was crafted by her mother, and clearly, my name wasn't meant to be in the final drawing. I should move on. She probably already has.

When I catch James's head poking through the curtains, I return the photo strip to my bag and tighten my coat to shield my neck from the chilling wind. Winters like this are making it difficult to stay in Seattle. Time to go inside.

The smell of melted cheese, rotisserie chicken, and hot sauce draws me toward the kitchen—and the homemade buffalo chicken dip, a reminder that home-cooked dishes still exist despite my empty refrigerator.

I smile at a picture hanging in the hallway—the four of us at the lake a year before Mamma passed. Despite the judgment we'd encounter from time to time, I had a great and loving childhood with a mother and two fathers. Out Black polyamorous families weren't a thing back then—not near us, anyway. But we were safe and always laughing about something. I'll never forget the overwhelming teamwork from both my dads after mom's car accident. Fuck drunk driving. I get my eyes from my mom, my height from my dad, and my stubbornness from James.

Turning the corner, I find James, apron hugging his big

belly, chopping celery, while Dad is organizing appetizers on the table. I watch them work as a team, seamlessly weaving around one another in the quaint kitchen.

Dad looks behind himself and his warm smile eases my mind. He drops the oven mitt onto the counter and pulls me into a bear hug, a stick of carrot dangling from his mouth. "Good to see you."

I feel another set of arms around us. A "King hug," we call it. "We've missed you so much, *and* you're just in time to help me finish cutting these carrots," James says as we separate, then gives Dad the eye. "Darrel keeps inviting more and more people, like we live in a mansion and have the budget to feed every queer in the city."

I laugh and set up another cutting board station next to James. Dad used to avoid gatherings like this, let alone host them. He really has changed since his military days.

"*So...*" James wastes no time being his typical nosy self. Meanwhile, Dad leaves to finish adding chairs near the TV. James does his signature dance before strategically inquiring about my love life. "How was the vacation?"

I continue chopping, strategizing short responses since the trip was work-related and also none of his business. "Not a vacation. I had to work. It went."

"Did you do anything fun?

"A few things."

"Meet anyone interesting?" I can feel his laser stare on me. "Say...a woman?"

Like clockwork. You'd think he was the private investigator in the family. I know he won't drop the topic unless I give him something. Or worse, he'll rope Dad into this, and I'll be outnumbered. "I met someone, but it didn't work out. Bad timing."

"Oh." He transfers his pile of cut carrots to the service platter.

Just when I think I won, he asks, "Did you...you know?" He forms scissor motions with his fingers and crosses them.

"James!" My cheeks ignite. I fail miserably to hide my smile before looking away. Admitting defeat, I crack up laughing. We've always had the type of relationship that most people wish they had with their parents, but sometimes it's a bit much. "You're worse than Kaydence."

"What?" He teases. "Clarifying questions are necessary. Do I look like an expert on the topic?"

I tilt my head and lower my voice. "Does a bear shit in the woods?"

The alto in his voice echoes as he laughs. "I'm not proud of everything that happened during my college years. Obviously you need to see her again. You're all wound up."

I playfully throw a top piece of carrot and giggle when it hits his shoulder. Taking a side step, I dodge the one catapulted in my direction.

"Okay. Okay. Last question: where is she from and was it serious?"

"That's *two* questions. She's from Seattle." I hesitate to finish my response. "I think it was serious." The truth comes out. "Yes, it was."

He gasps with a teasing grin. "*You're* in Seattle. So, we're good on location but bad on timing? That's an easy fix."

Since when is poor timing ever easy? The fact that I took the case not knowing Basil was my target until *after* we slept together is proof. Not quitting the case sooner and telling her the truth? More proof. I leave out the specifics.

"For now." I finish cutting the last carrot and rinse the knife. "Actually, I've been thinking about a change of scenery. Maybe the East Coast."

"Babe!" James yells. "Come talk to your daughter. She's trying to leave again. And there's a *woman*." He shifts his attention and whispers, "What's her name?"

I open my mouth but get saved by the doorbell.

"Hang on." Dad's heavy footsteps drift further away. "Grabbing the door," he calls. "Liz and Tate are outside. We'll be there in a hot second."

We? Damn it. I groan and slap my forehead.

James wiggles his eyebrows in victory. "Now it's a party."

Seven doorbell rings later…

I was supposed to leave this house an hour ago. Instead, I'm sitting in front of the TV, officially starring in tonight's entertainment. There's so much screaming, clapping, and fun debating happening right now, you'd think it was game night.

Despite the fact that my love life is being attacked by well-meaning, but clueless friends and family, I can't ignore the warmth in my heart from all of the support.

If this many people want the best for me—to follow my heart, why shouldn't I?

A loud whistle from Dad quiets the room for James to be heard.

"I just have one question: what are you waiting for?" James finally says, and everyone fixes their attention to me. You love her, right?" He hands me my coat and rushes me to the front door. "You're a King. We don't wait for good timing, we create good timing."

Back inside the car, I pull the photo-booth strip out again. Lynn's words come to mind. I wonder if there's a chance that Basil believes we have a future worth more pictures. I guess there's only one way to find out.

An idea strikes me. I retrieve my phone and call Kaydence.

When she answers, I blurt out the words before she finishes greeting me. "How about one last job? Please."

My lips curl into a smile when she accepts.

"I'll tell you everything later, but first, I need an address."

CHAPTER 30

BASIL

"It's lovely to see you again, dear," Mae tells me while adjusting her sun hat and dress so that Lynn can fit into the camera frame. They appear to be sitting in chairs on top of a balcony. I attempt to curb my envy of their perfect mid-morning weather while it's still a dull, wintry night here. Memories of the island's clean air are taking me back to Caroline's and my beach date. I can almost smell the aroma of the salty sea breeze and baking sand.

"Happy Monday." Lynn waves hello once she's settled beside Mae, sunglasses resting on top of her head. "Mondays might not be many people's favorite, but I've always loved them. Fresh starts and all that."

"It's easy to feel that way when you're living on an island and only go into the office whenever it suits you." Mae gives her wife a knowing smile, then faces me. "We'll be considerate since we heard there's a risk of snow in Seattle."

"Which is uncommon, so that means the city will come to halt. The good news is it doesn't last long. Plus, I have tea to keep me warm." I hold up my mug.

After I answer their questions about my company's

customer success process, they go off screen for a moment. According to Lynn, Quilliam wants to say hello, so she went to retrieve him.

The Blakemans and I have been working together for over six months now, and not once have either of them brought up Caroline. I've been dreading that moment, knowing I have to continue letting them believe in my fake marriage—a consequence of the wine deal.

I sit with my thoughts and can't help but wonder: why hasn't Lynn asked about Caroline?

Did Victoria tell them? I recall our conversation at the airport—the Blakemans seem to enjoy working with my company. Yet, I've been dishonest in my strongest client relationship to date—with people I've come to care about immensely. Is this the type of businesswoman I am now? Then again, maybe they'd understand. Or should I simply say that Caroline and I didn't work out? Technically, that's true. My heart sinks at the thought of speaking those words out loud. I miss her.

Exhaling, I unplug the electric kettle and pour hot water into my mug. Obtaining the wine deal was a part of my job, and I'm proud of that accomplishment, at least.

I wish this indecisiveness inside me would end. Deep down, I want to tell them the truth. I can't believe I let Mother's words of caution about ruining the relationship intimidate me.

"Basil?" Mae repeats.

I snap back to reality and return my gaze to the screen. They're back. Quilliam too. "I'm sorry. My mind has been occupied lately."

"So, uh, any meaningful developments?" Lynn's eyes shift side to side. "With a certain someone?"

Mae scolds Lynn with a glare. I scramble to understand

what she's talking about, but then I sense who that "certain someone" is.

No more lying.

I straighten my back. "Actually, there's something I need to tell both of you. Caroline and I aren't…" Pause. "We're not…" I'm struggling to get the words out. Admitting it out loud means my relationship with Caroline is really over. "We're not—"

"Married?" Lynn peers over at Mae, then back to me. "We know."

The heat drains from my face. My mouth opens and closes, but no words come out. "You do?"

"We're old, not dumb, dear," Mae says matter-of-factly.

"How is this possible?" I blurt the words before I have a chance to stop them. "Did she tell you?" Hell, maybe everyone knows Caroline's a private investigator but me?

"No," Lynn responds. "I social-media stalked you the night we saw you and Caroline together in the resort restaurant and put two and two together. You were acting pretty strange for a newlywed couple. I figured you might have taken issue with Quilliam, but then I thought maybe there's more to this than meets the eye."

With the chaotic wedding, updating online profile pictures was the last thing on my mind. I blink twice in disbelief. Nevermind the damn hedgehog right now. "You've known the entire time?"

"Pretty certain we have." Mae winces. "Sorry. We didn't want to get involved in your personal matters. We assumed you had your reasons."

Lynn snorts a laugh. "What do I look like? Psychic or something? I assumed you and Caroline had some type of friend-agreement. You know, like in the movies."

Speechless, I slide both hands over my face. What a mess. "I'm sorry for lying. Are you upset?"

"It was highly unnecessary on your part. We could've easily rescheduled. But ultimately, no. We love drama. Especially when it's not ours," Mae says with a half grin. "It's understandable that your agreement ended and you had to 'break up.' I will say though, from the start, I thought you two would be a stunning couple."

*You and me both...*I shake my head. I feel like a complete fool.

"Mae and I even made a little bet on getting you and Caroline to kiss. She won."

Lynn's teasing grin and shoulders bouncing up and down as she chuckles tells me the story behind Caroline's and my kiss on the beach. Happy Monday.

There's nothing left for me to say but the truth. I start from the beginning—getting left at the altar. Mother's blueprint. Caroline. Once I started talking, I spill everything out and then some.

Later, I say, "Sapphire Isle is incredible, and I fell in love while I was there. That wasn't a part of the plan. Now, I don't know what to do. I can't stop thinking about her." I take a breath through my raw emotions. Certainly the Blakemans see how unprofessional this conversation is. "I'm sorry. I shouldn't be saying—"

"Don't apologize." Mae softens in a way I've never seen before. "We wanted to work with Elixir Wines because of you, not your mother. Failed ploys aside, you're the one that shares alignment with our vision, and you're the amazing businesswoman that keeps us invested. You remind me of myself when I was your age."

"If you ever want to come work with us, just say the word. It's a done deal. We're near the second phase of expansion and we're looking for a Chief of Marketing if you're interested in a career transition. We can discuss relocation packages anytime."

Work for the Blakemans? I can't believe how this call started to where we are now.

Warmth radiates through my entire body. I'd love to work for the them. "That'd be incredible and a great honor, but you don't have to do that. I—"

"No rush. This is your decision. No one else's."

Being cherry-picked from my family business seems like a low move to make.

Returning my focus to the screen, I raise my chin. "Can I think about it? I need to figure out what's best for me."

Mae nods with a grin. I can tell she respects my decision. "Offer's open."

The call ends. I log off and lean back in my chair, still shocked at what just happened. As amazing as living on an island sounds, would I be happy working for someone else?

And then, I can't ignore the joy I'm feeling at this moment —a taste of creating my own blueprint.

Two mouse clicks and I'm eye to eye with a blank document on my word processor. I stare at the blinking cursor and rest my fingers on the keys.

This isn't because Mother hired Caroline in the first place or because I'm accepting the Blakemans' offer. This is for me. Maybe love's not enough, but now I know I am. What Caroline and I shared proves it even more.

It's time I retire from the wine business. I begin typing, and each word feels like I'm winning a round of the Sapphic Olympics all over again.

I am writing to formally notify you of my resignation...

CHAPTER 31

CAROLINE

"There it is," I say to myself when I locate the house. I appreciate that Kaydence was able to complete my request to find Basil's address, given her busy schedule with two children now. Downtown rush hour traffic is picking up, so I grab the first available parking space two houses down and successfully maneuver my sedan parallel on the street. Once I turn off the ignition, I grip the wheel tightly, inhale a breath, and let it out slowly. The plan has to work. It might not make up for my deception in the first place, but at least I can finally tell Basil how I feel, even after several months apart. This could go one of two ways: fantastically, or horribly, miserably wrong. Hopefully she's home. I'm all out of moves.

I think about everything that has led me to this moment, unable to deny the fact that something inside my heart zinged back to life when I fell for Basil. Perhaps I've always been good enough for love, I had just been giving the best parts of me to the wrong people.

Despite the temperature inside the car dropping, I wipe my sweaty palms on my jeans. I dig through my bag and remove the items I hope will redeem me a second chance. One more deep breath, and I exit my car.

I wrap my plaid scarf around my neck, steeling myself. I trek through the cold toward the tan building while I rehearse what I'm going to say for the hundredth time.

As I ascend the steps, my heart pounds in my throat and I hope that the woman I fell head over heels for can love me. *This is different. Don't think about the past,* I remind myself and push thoughts of rejection far from my mind.

At the top, I bump into a heavy cardboard box with a shipping label plastered across one side. I carefully push it to the side with my boot. The lump in my throat grows with each second, my mind whirling with thousands of unspoken words. I go to knock on the door, but freeze the moment I see activity through the gap between the curtains. I blink.

I see Basil. It's her—wait.

A cold disbelief washes over me, numbing all of my senses. She's on the couch watching TV, arm draped around another woman—now *kissing* another woman. Her brunette hair is pinned up in the ponytail I remember.

My shoulders sink. My view is restricted, but what I'm witnessing is clear. Basil doesn't want to be with me.

Feet frozen in place, I watch as they kiss again. I hear familiar laughter—sounds that drive a knife deeper into my heart.

I knock anyway. Two hard taps.

What am I doing? I pull my hand away. What do I expect to happen next? Am I going to greet her girlfriend? I place the envelope on top of the box—bearing someone else's name—on the door and accept defeat. Love's not for me. I stumble backward, propelled by an overwhelming urge to leave Seattle and Basil's and my future behind. The photo-booth strip falls from my hand onto the ground.

The thin layer of snow crunches underneath my boots,

and each step releases a tear down my cheeks. What was I thinking, coming here? I refuse to look back. I don't swivel around to check if anyone answered the door. It doesn't matter. Basil has moved on.

Lynn's words come to mind. *At least you won't have to wonder.* There's no point in pondering ways to get her back either. She's moved on. Maybe I should too.

Everything hurts like hell right now. My car feels like it's twenty houses away, not two. When I finally reach my vehicle on the side of the street, I continue walking. I'm so heartbroken, the last thing I want to do is drive.

CHAPTER 32

BASIL

"I THOUGHT you two agreed to help me pack?" I wipe the sweat forming on my temples. It might be winter outside, but it feels like the peak of summer inside the house. I'm wearing an old, weathered gray T-shirt and black yoga pants—-the only clothes that remain unpacked, ones that would otherwise never see the light of day. I'm not leaving this house unless it's an emergency. Hand on my hip, I squint a glare toward my sister and Riley cuddling on the couch. "I swear you two act like a couple of love-drunk teenagers. Always hiding away or watching movies and groping each other." Watching them reminds me of how Caroline and I acted. She brought out a playful side of me that hasn't emerged since our time on the island.

"Sorry." Hazel pauses the TV and jumps to her feet. Her hair is getting long. It's only a matter of time until she'll get it cut short again. "I thought we were taking a break."

My brow slants upward. "For two hours?" I love them both, but—no but, *and* thank god I'm moving out of this love shack.

I ask again. Nicer this time. "Oh, kind people. *Whenever*

you're free, I'd appreciate your assistance." I'm not being sarcastic, but my tone indicates otherwise. After all, they did volunteer to help me pack since the movers canceled at the last minute due to inclement weather. Nearly every business in this city seems to shut down at the mere thought of snow.

"How are things going upstairs?" Hazel asks, retrieving more empty boxes from the kitchen floor. "Are you two getting along?"

I offer a confident nod. "We had to iron out a couple of nuances, other than that, yes. I've never seen our mother work so hard to earn anyone's trust." Repairing issues between us may take months, years even, but we're off to a decent-ish start. When the movers canceled, Mother advised that with a little bonus money, she could get two men onsite in minutes. I refused and asked if she would help me move the old-fashioned way—pizza, sweat, and good people— instead of throwing money at problems. Hearing the word "no" seems foreign to her, but I've learned a thing or two about setting boundaries this year, and more so what happens when there are none.

She hardly put up a fight when I stepped into her office and handed in my resignation letter. I wasn't sure if guilt for hiring Caroline caught up with her was the reason or maybe she knew how miserable I had become. I never thought I'd quit Elixir Wines, but I'm glad I did. For the first time, I feel in charge of my life. But thoughts of what I said to Caroline still haunt me.

"Did the mail come?" Riley sets a box on the coffee table and tapes it closed. "I'm supposed to get new fabric today."

I push the box in front of the TV. Hopefully they get the hint.

"I think I heard the delivery person knock earlier, but I was too lazy to get up," Hazel says from the living room.

I slide my slippers on and pull the front door open. I

shiver at the frigid breeze and bend down to retrieve the box. The package is Riley's. There's another one. *What's this?* I pick up the envelope propped up on its side, and something sticking out of the ground catches my attention.

I flip the thin strip over. I cover my mouth with a hand and immediately become misty-eyed. It's the photo-booth pictures of me and Caroline. I tug at the envelope and pull out the paper inside. That's Caroline's handwriting. My heart pounds as I frantically shield the sheet from the wind and read it. Title: *Basil and Caroline's Honeymoon Itinerary—for real this time.*

The itinerary is blank. I turn the sheet around to the other side. My chin wobbles as I read the *How We Met* section —the bar in Seattle. There are more sections, marked with *TBD.*

A note is at the bottom of the page.

Basil,

Our honeymoon mix-up was the best thing that ever happened to me.

I believe we're worth a future of more pictures. More memories. More laughs and arguments and kisses. A real chance at love. I want to fill this out together one day if you'll have me. I'm so sorry for hurting you. I love you and I miss you terribly.

—Caroline

"I love you too," I whisper, a single tear rolling down my cheek. Where is she? I look around. All I see are yellow taxis and cars and people bundled in heavy coats pacing the streets. But not one of them is Caroline King. Why'd she leave? She probably left to respect the distance she thinks I want.

I step back inside, still able to see my breath in the entry-way. I walk over to tell Hazel and Riley, but pause and peer out the living room window. It hits me. I was wrong. She probably saw Hazel and Riley and thought it was me, then left needing space to process what she saw.

I see a familiar silhouette inside of a taxi rolling past. Caroline? It has to be. Adrenaline rushes through my veins. There's no time to get dressed. I drop Riley's package and bolt out the door. No jacket. No hat. No shoes. Only desperation to stop Caroline from leaving before it's too late.

With the photo-booth pictures clenched tightly in my grip, I soar down the steps. When I hit the last one, I slip and fall forward, bouncing off a couple that happens to be walking past, then I land on the ground. I groan in pain. Four sets of hands reach to help, but I wave them away. I struggle and return to my feet. My entire side is soaked from the sloshy sidewalk.

Ignoring the cold air piercing my skin, I find the taxi and begin my dash once more, fueled by fear.

Traffic is speeding up, but with these slippers promising another fall, I can only go so fast. My heart pounds against my chest. I'm panting. My hair is sticking up in every direction. I have no clue when my hair tie fell.

I shout at the cars. "Stop!" But it's futile. People are staring as I shove past, but I couldn't care less. This is for love.

She's the missing piece to my blueprint.

Just when I think I've lost Caroline, her taxi halts at the red light not far ahead. The one time in my life I'll praise this ridiculous street light that takes forever. This is not my finest moment. My hair is sticking to my forehead, and I refuse to think about the source of that smell.

I reach the passenger window, struggling to steady my breath, ready to pour out my heart and soul. My face drops. *What?*

This person isn't Caroline. I'm crushed.

Is it too late?

My heart breaks into pieces like it did the first time in the villa—no, worse. The person I need is the one person I may never see again. I never asked for her phone number. I wish I could tell her how much I want another try. Feet drenched and freezing, I ignore the honking cars and go to the sidewalk. My head remains pointed down, and I make my way back toward the house.

"Basil?" I hear a familiar voice. My pulse jumps, and I look up.

Caroline? My eyes lock on hers. She's standing right in front of me, not inside a taxi. I huff a laugh. My entire body beams with relief, warmth, and a renewed sense of hope.

I'm certain that in my disheveled state, I look like I've gotten into a fight with blender, but I don't care. She's here.

Enamored, I approach her. The world I know fades away. The snow, the traffic, the cutting wind. Whatever this stench is. None of it matters. In front of me is the woman I want to spend my life with.

I smile and wipe the tears away. "Hi. You're the most beautiful woman I've ever seen. Can I buy you coffee sometime?"

Please say yes.

The silence is excruciating. Months have passed since we've seen each other, but it feels like years.

I swallow the lump in my throat and search her eyes for answers. I don't know if she's staring at me because she's repulsed or happy.

Remembering why she may have left, I clarify, "That was my sister back there, my *identical* twin sister. Not me."

Even though she hasn't said a word, her relief is almost palpable, a beacon of hope that she believes me. What feels like years later, I see the tight grip on her phone loosen.

Our gazes hold. The only thing I can hear at this moment is her silence.

A shaky sigh escapes her lips, followed by a soft, almost incredulous chuckle. I can't help but laugh too.

I know this is a lot to take in. I take her soft hand into mine. "I don't want a life without you in it. You showed me what true love looks like. I've spent the last seven months trying to build a new life, but I've come to realize that what was missing all along was you." I hold out my other hand and open it. The now-crinkled strip of photos rests in my palm. "Caroline, we're worth a million more pictures. I love you."

Her big beautiful smile relaxes my shoulders. She pulls me into her arms and hugs me tight and my heart illuminates with joy and happiness. I never want to let go. "Two vanilla dirty chai lattes sound perfect." She tilts my chin and presses our lips together for a tender kiss. "I love you too."

EPILOGUE

CAROLINE

Eight months later.

"That's way more than seven seconds," Basil whispers against my lips and kisses me. Her smile widens against mine, making my entire body beam with love.

"Can you blame me?" I peck her again and pull back just enough to speak. "My wife is pretty hot."

She giggles, a flair of pink on her cheeks. I love making her blush.

Seated beside me on the deck floor, she intertwines our fingers together and lets out a satisfied sigh. "This perfect weather is exactly what we needed. I missed this place so much."

I inhale, filling my lungs with the crisp ocean breeze, and exhale slowly. My muscles relax when I drink in my gorgeous wife. "Me too." I stretch my legs out on the deck floor while we enjoy our breathtaking view of the endless miles of crystal-blue water.

My cheeks are sore from all the smiling we've been doing since exchanging vows yesterday. I couldn't imagine a more perfect day, surrounded by an immense amount of love and happiness.

It was Basil's idea to have a destination wedding. I smile to myself. We even gained an inside running joke that she married me on an island for a reason—that way I couldn't get away. But I was proud to be standing there on the beach, the sunset and our past heartbreak behind us. Everything about Basil makes me appreciate life more. Given our journey, I'll take the feelings in my heart for granted. Not now. Not ever. I love Basil.

"Dinner at 6 p.m.?" I ask and bring her fingers to my mouth and plant a tender kiss across her knuckles.

She nods and snuggles up against me.

"Okay. I'll text Kaydence in a bit and let her know." I remember when I broke the news about out where we wanted to Honeymoon to Kaydence and her wife and how loud they cheered when they found out they could come too.

Since we have a few hours left until dinner, I reach for my bag and pull out a notebook binder and set it on my lap. Our itinerary.

Basil yanks it away, a playful curl in her lips. "I'm going to need to cross stuff out aren't I? You probably added more meal breaks so we have more of those than the other events combined."

"Not unless you can get it." I steal the binder back and chuckle at Basil's failed attempts to reach up my long arms. She climbs on top of me and straddles my waist. Our eyes lock. Seeing hers full of emotion, the butterflies swarm in my belly. "I love you so much." She dips down and brushes our lips together.

I deepen the kiss, my mind traveling back in time to all the intimacy shared between us on this same deck. My heart warms knowing how far we've come and how we didn't give up on love. Our feelings for one another were real, even if the relationship status was not.

Held captive underneath her thighs, I pull her close and kiss her passionately. Taking advantage of my distracted state, using two fingers, she pulls the binder from my hand.

Basil smiles and takes a moment to read the first page—the summary. Meanwhile I'm struggling to suppress my giggle.

When finished, she gives me a look. "Hedgehog Olympics? How long does that even last? Five minutes?" The look on her face is priceless. "You're telling me there's *multiple* of those things on this island?"

I finally burst with a deep belly laughter. "We have to cheer Quilliam on. You know Lynn will appreciate the support. Like she and Mae did for us."

She grumbles something underneath her breath. "I can say that attending the Hedgehog Olympics was definitely not on my version of the honeymoon itinerary. But you're right." She makes a contemplative sound. "Quilliam is kind of cute. Don't tell Lynn I said that."

"I won't unless you're ready to hold him." I crack a laugh.

"Absolutely not." She shakes her head with a grin and points at the binder again. "Also, you sure love to exercise. It's listed almost every day."

"Excuse me, Mrs. King-Jones, horizontal exercise counts."

She playfully sticks her tongue out and our gaze holds. She is so beautiful. I'm incredibly lucky.

Her eyes drifts to my lips, then back up. She lowers her voice to a whisper. "Say that again."

Completely enamored, I lean closer until our lips are an inch apart. "Mrs. King-Jones." Given the way she's looking at me, Kaydence and Nikita might have to eat dinner without us because there's something else I'm craving to sink my teeth into about now. But I can wait. I want to savor the moment.

"I'll never get tired of hearing that name." Basil's words brings me back from my naughty thought. "I adore it." We lock lips again. "Especially at the family Thanksgiving football tournament."

We share a laugh and I bump my fist against hers. "You just like to remind the rest of the Joneses that you're a champion. I hope you're happy."

Basil looks at me with that beautiful dimpled-grin that I love. "How can I not be? I scored the highest prize in the world." She kisses my lips. "You."

* * *

Want to see how Basil and Caroline are doing and a year from now? Get your free BONUS EPILOGUE today! It has your favorite characters and a spicy adult prom night you won't forget ;)

Bonus Epilogue
subscribepage.com/thehoneymoonmixup-bonus

GET A FREE BOOK

Join us!

When you sign up for my mailing list, you'll get new release updates, bonuses, giveaways and more! You'll also get a FREE copy of *Doing Summer Right,* my erotic romance novella when joining. <3

https://www.subscribepage.com/frankiefyrenewsletter

DOING SUMMER RIGHT

SNEAK PEEK - CHAPTER 1

With one last glide of the paddle, the kayak crashed onto the pebbled shore. Hazel took a deep breath, stretching her arms over her head, and added a satisfied exhale before tossing the double-bladed oar to the ground. Another perfect morning on the water. Nothing was more soothing than the rhythmic lull of floating, surrounded by near crystal bluish-green ripples and an earthy scent to start your day. Some people practiced yoga, some meditated or journaled for their solace. Hazel Jones paddled.

After stepping out of the kayak, she pulled it further up the rocks to ensure it wouldn't drift away before walking toward the main cabin. She was practically raised on the water of Lake Tamoa, a hidden gem outside of Tenton, Florida. For as long as she could remember, she stayed from June through the end of July until completing her undergrad. After being accepted into med school, she'd moved to the city, only to realize six years later that her love for animals and nature exceeded her love for people. So, she quit her job and moved back.

Despite all the trouble, everything worked out. Hazel got to live where she wanted for free. Well, almost free. She owned the cabin in exchange for helping her aunt run her business as lead facilities manager, overseeing supply inventory and upkeep of the grounds. Examining the campsite, Hazel made a mental note to fix the lopsided *Complete Minds Complete Bodies* sign by the entrance, after breakfast. There were two days left before all hell broke loose—the next wave of people arriving for summer camp.

Walking through the cabin door, she tossed her life jacket on a hook and followed her nose to the kitchen. Pausing at the flour shoe prints across the floor, she leaned against the door frame, arms folded. Hazel cracked a smile as her best friend, Riley Davis, made a mess of her cabin. She had arrived yesterday and was already taking over her space. Riley was the assistant director and she led camp orientations.

The entire cabin smelled delicious with the perfect mixture of savory and sweet, and her favorite: bacon and waffles. Unfortunately, Riley's efforts in the cooking department were almost always better than the results, but that never stopped her from trying.

"At least nothing is burning this time." Hazel said, giggling as Riley jolted into the air.

Wide-eyed, Riley whipped around to face her, tongs pointed like a dagger. "Jesus, Hazel, you scared me." Flashing a playful glare at her comment, she handed her the plate of bacon, knowing well where she was headed. "Don't worry; I found the perfect ingredient to launch my waffle recipe to the next level."

"Chocolate chips? Honey?" Hazel asked as she set a plate on the counter. From behind, she draped her arms over Riley's shoulders. A shorter woman, Riley was the perfect height for hugs, amongst other things.

Hazel's mouth found her ear and whispered, "You know, if you wanted something sweet to taste, all you had to do was ask." She kissed her cheek, exaggerating an audible smack.

"Don't start something you can't finish, Hazel," she said, moving her voluminous, coily hair, tempting her by tilting her head and giving access to her neck. "If I recall, your to-do list is full. Isn't that what you were complaining about last night?"

"I could use the distraction. Would you like to be added to the top?"

She held a hand up, halting the air. "We *both* have a busy day. Besides, I thought I called the shots around here?"

Without responding, Hazel swiped a finger along the rim of the cookie butter jar and pretended to feed her. Falling for the trick, Riley opened her mouth wide, only for her to dot her nose instead.

She huffed, removing the dollop with a finger and licking it clean. Wearing her cute 'thinking' face, Riley touched her chin. "Although hazelnut-spread waffles topped with whipped cream and strawberries sounds pretty amazing. I think we have the ingredients if you want to help."

"Are we talking about food or something else?" Hazel asked, amused at the way Riley squinted with pursed lips.

"Hazel plus spread, plus whipped cream, equals a fantastic time."

"Too bad I'm allergic to nuts," Riley quipped.

"Perfect. Me too."

She shot Hazel a look. "Are we *still* talking about food or something else?"

They burst out laughing as Riley slapped her arm and wiggled out of her embrace. Grabbing the mixing bowl and remote, Riley turned the volume up on the TV. Best friends, they had a fairly unorthodox relationship. Harmonious and entertaining, coated with a hint of sexual tension. They'd tried to date a couple of years back, but Riley taught her that loving someone and being compatible with their lifestyle choices are two entirely different things. Not to mention, Hazel was a tad bit of a control freak.

After less than six months of dating, they realized they made better friends than lovers. Friends that, every once in a while, shared an intimate night together. Nothing official, only a mutual understanding to do what felt natural during her impromptu visits. Times when she craved more than what others were willing to give. Hell, most times, they just enjoyed poking fun at each other.

Hazel stabbed the top waffle on the stack with her fork, halting when her nose scrunched from the lingering scent of egg. Thinking better of it, she stuck to the bacon, secretly tossing the offending food in the trash bin.

"I know it's your last year as assistant director, but you really don't have to go above and beyond by making a fancy breakfast for everyone. The kids love the make-your-own pancake bar. If it ain't broke..." she said. Riley had amazing qualities. Cooking waffles wasn't one of them.

Riley pointed at the TV. "I found a cooking show that doesn't make me want to fall asleep. And, check this episode out. This chef *only* cooks breakfast. If I can't learn how to make perfect waffles from her, I quit."

"Found yourself a miracle worker, yeah?" Hazel teased, grabbing a third piece of bacon. Her eyes landed on the screen, and her heart stopped for a moment. "Holy shit."

Riley squealed with excitement, throwing her arms in the air. "Smoking hot, right? I can't wait to meet her."

"Meet who? *Her?*"

"Didn't you see the email? Your aunt sent it last week."

"What email?"

"I swear, woman. If you didn't have me, you'd never

interact with another human again." Riley pushed her phone in Hazel's face. "Summer Bedingfield is staying *here* for three days. She volunteered to give free cooking lessons to the campers. Arrives tomorrow, I believe."

This time, Hazel pointed at the TV. "*That* Summer Bedingfield?"

Riley nodded, eyes trailing the beautiful cherry-lipstick-wearing redhead pacing around the southern-style kitchen. Even the host seemed to sneak a lingering glance when she turned to pull a hand towel from the drawer, stuffing it in her back pocket. "What I'd give to be that towel right now." Riley sighed, then shook her head. "Wait, didn't you go to school with her? I think I read that in the email."

Hazel hesitated before responding. Some people just had worldly success written all over them. Forgetting a woman like Summer Bedingfield was near impossible. Hell, she'd tried. "No, not school. Summer camp, actually. She and I were my aunt's interns for a season. She said she'd return, but she moved back to Atlanta. Her dad had a hotel franchise headquartered there."

"What was she like?"

"Honestly, I don't remember much." After telling a white lie, her eyes found the TV again. Summer Bedingfield was as captivating as a rare creature in the wild, and from what she remembered, had quite the personality. Returning to reality, she gave Riley a little more before being called out for staring. "She's obviously a head-turner. And about as southern sweet as ice tea without the sugar."

Riley snorted. "That bad?"

"Ironically, her name is Summer, but she is the biggest ice queen I have ever met. At least she was back then. She looks much friendlier on TV so, perhaps the camera softened her up."

Riley danced her fingers up Hazel's forearm. With a teasing tone, she asked, "Did she get under the famous Hazel Jones's skin?"

"Just about as much as your cooking skills."

Jaw hanging, Riley flicked flour in her face. "All right, out of my kitchen. And don't come crawling to me at lunchtime. Riley Eatery is closed." Raising her eyebrow, she put her hands on her hips. "*All* of Riley Eatery."

"Good thing I know just the thing to warm you back up to fire on all cylinders." Hazel pinned her with a confident gaze, picked up the last piece of bacon, and placed it in front of her mouth.

"You're lucky we're best friends," she said.

"We agree on one thing at least. I am *extremely* lucky."

"Too late, tiger, don't be a kiss ass. Now, out you go." Riley chomped on the bacon, thankfully missing Hazel's finger, and pointed toward the exit. Laughing to herself, she walked out the door, grabbing the hammer and box of two-inch nails out of the desk drawer. Back to work. "That sign isn't going to fix itself," she grumbled, and made her way toward the entrance.

She glanced at her list for the next task. *Replace flood light bulb at cabin 10.* Her head shifted to the cabin Summer Bedingfield and she had shared, along with the memories. Memories that teased her thoughts more than once over the years. She was certain that the famous woman had long forgotten her name and face, let alone what Summer had said. But not Hazel.

You never forget the first time your fingers explore a woman's wetness. Or the first time she tastes yours. And certainly not her promises of more.

Next time, the memory of a sultry, whispering voice echoed in her mind. A portent—good or evil? The promise

Summer Bedingfield made on the last night before she left almost ten years ago. *Next time, you're mine.*

To Be Continued…
Get Free Book
subscribepage.com/frankiefyrenewsletter

A NOTE FROM FRANKIE

Dear reader

Thank you for reading this book! If you enjoyed the story, I would greatly appreciate your help with spreading the word so others can too. How, you ask?

Honest reviews help authors tremendously and as an independent author who writes fiction for a smaller niche market, word of mouth and reviews are two of the best ways that encourage readers all over the world to give me a try and enjoy my books.

If you'd like, feel free to leave a review on Goodreads and/or the retailer's site where you purchased the book. No worries on the length. Just a couple of sentences makes a huge impact and helps keep the lights on.

Thank you for your kindness and thank you so much for growing with me! :)

ALSO BY FRANKIE FYRE

A Flight to Love

Doing Summer Right

ABOUT THE AUTHOR

Thank you for reading!

Sign up for Frankie's newsletter for updates on her latest books.

Frankie Fyre is an author, reader and foodie—*especially* tacos. She adores writing tropey, fun and spicy Sapphic romance centered around memorable diverse characters, delicious tension, and happily ever afters.

When she's not writing kissing books, she can be found reading, making people laugh, trying new food and hanging out with her lovely partner.

You can connect with Frankie on social media and follow her Amazon page for release updates.

amazon.com/Frankie-Fyre/e/B09957395K
bookbub.com/authors/frankie-fyre
x.com/frankiefyre
instagram.com/frankiefyrewriter

Printed in Dunstable, United Kingdom